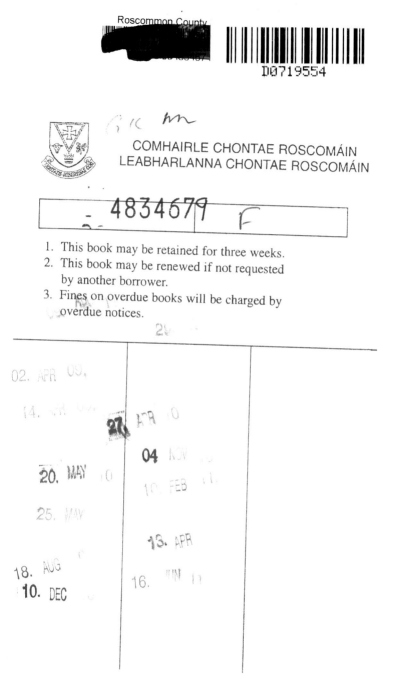

Do you ever wish you could
step into someone else's shoes?

IN HER SHOES...

Now you can with Mills & Boon Romance®'s
new miniseries brimming full of
contemporary, feel-good stories.

Our modern day Cinderellas
swap glass slippers for a stylish stiletto!

So follow each footstep through makeover to
marriage, rags to riches, as these women
fulfill their hopes and dreams....

**Step into Sophie's shoes
and watch in wonder as
the housekeeper becomes the bride in:**

**Maid in Montana
by
Susan Meier
June 2009**

Out of the corner of her eye she could see the firm line of his jaw and the corner of that mouth. He wasn't smiling, but there was a dent in his cheek and a quirk to the set of his lips that sent warmth shivering through her. She tried looking away and staring at his jacket instead, but the material seemed to shimmer in front of her gaze after a while and her eyes slid surreptitiously back to his mouth.

It was so close. All he had to do was turn his head just a little, and if she turned hers too their lips would meet. What would that be like? The answer came in the leap of her heart, the acceleration of her pulse at the very thought, and Miranda closed her eyes against the instinctive knowledge of how thrilling it would be to touch her lips to his, to feel his mouth take sure, seductive possession of hers.

He would be a very good kisser. He had had lots of practice, after all. Miranda dragged the feverish drift of her thoughts back to reality. What was she thinking? That Rafe Knighton, playboy extraordinaire, would actually think about kissing *her*? He had his pick of beautiful women. Was it really likely that he would pass them all over in favour of plain Miranda Fairchild?

CINDERELLA'S WEDDING WISH

BY
JESSICA HART

MILLS & BOON®
Pure reading pleasure™

First published in Great Britain 2009
Harlequin Mills & Boon Limited,
Eton House, 18-24 Paradise Road, Richmond, Surrey TW9 1SR

© Jessica Hart 2009

ISBN: 978 0 263 20705 7

Set in Times Roman 10½ on 13 pt
07-0109-43513

Printed and bound in Great Britain
by CPI Antony Rowe, Chippenham, Wiltshire

Jessica Hart was born in West Africa, and has suffered from itchy feet ever since, travelling and working around the world in a wide variety of interesting but very lowly jobs, all of which have provided inspiration on which to draw when it comes to the settings and plots of her stories. Now she lives a rather more settled existence in York, where she has been able to pursue her interest in history, although she still yearns sometimes for wider horizons. If you'd like to know more about Jessica, visit her website www.jessicahart.co.uk

CHAPTER ONE

'OH, FOR heaven's sake!' Miranda yanked impatiently at the front of the photocopier and banged it open so that she could peer inside. '*Now* what?' she demanded. 'I've cleared the jam, I've refilled all the paper trays… I can't believe you really need toner too! You're just being difficult.'

Exasperated, she shoved her hand into the machine to release the catch for the toner cartridge, only to catch her finger on a protruding piece of machinery. Jerking back with a yelp, she let out an involuntary exclamation. Miranda didn't normally swear but it would have taken a saint not to lose it after the morning she had had with this machine.

She glared at the photocopier. 'Right, that's *it*! I've had enough of you now!'

Shaking her stinging finger and too frustrated to think what else to do, Miranda aimed a childish kick at the photocopier with another muttered exclamation.

'Language, language!' A tutting sound from behind her made Miranda's head snap round.

A man was lounging in the doorway of the copying room, grinning at her. And not just any man. He was impossibly handsome, with dark hair, glinting navy blue eyes, the kind of features a male model would kill for and a smile perfectly designed to set most female hearts a-flutter.

Not Miranda's though. Her heart didn't do fluttering. Maybe it skipped, just a little, at the sight of him, but that was just surprise.

That was what she told herself anyway.

She had never met him before, but she knew exactly who he was, of course. There was no mistaking him. Rafe Knighton, darling of the gossip columnists, and the new Chairman and Chief Executive of the Knighton Group, which technically made him her boss.

And the last person she would have expected to encounter in the copying room, exuding assurance and glamour. The tall, dark and handsome cliché might have been invented for Rafe Knighton, she thought, determinedly unimpressed. He was immaculately dressed in a beautifully cut suit that fitted perfectly across his broad shoulders. His shirt was a luxuriously plain white, his tie discreet, classy, and knotted with just the right combination of ease and elegance. Miranda would have liked to dismiss him as effeminate, but at close quarters it was all too obvious that there was nothing effete about Rafe Knighton. He was all too solidly male.

Briefly, she wondered what he was doing slumming it on the communications floor. Perhaps he strolled down every few days to thrill the staff with his presence, and amused himself by seeing how long it took the females to swoon at his feet.

If he was waiting for her to do the same, he was in for a long wait, boss or no boss.

On the other hand, being caught swearing and kicking the office equipment probably wasn't the best way to endear herself to the management, Miranda reflected. A swoon might be a better option. It was that, or brazen it out.

Before she had a chance to decide, Rafe Knighton had straightened from the doorway and was strolling into the room as if he owned it.

Which he did, of course.

'I've a good mind to report you to the Royal Society for the Prevention of Cruelty to Photocopiers!' he said, wagging a chastising finger at her. 'That poor machine shouldn't have to put up with that kind of language, when it can't answer back.'

The deadpan delivery was contradicted by the dancing humour in his eyes and ripple of amusement in his voice. The man practically *oozed* charm, Miranda thought, annoyed that she still had to brace herself to resist it.

As if she didn't have enough to annoy her at the moment.

It was too late to swoon, anyway.

'The photocopier started it,' she said coldly.

Rafe's eyes gleamed as he studied her. He was still getting used to the idea that Knighton's wealth and prestige was his responsibility now, and the realisation could be oppressive at times. Whenever he started feeling that the walls were closing in on him, he took a walk. He told everyone that he wanted to familiarise himself with the company, which was true, but Rafe knew that these tours of the building were more about his own restlessness and inability to decide whether he had done the right thing in coming back.

Knighton's was an institution, with a fiercely loyal and dedicated staff, and Rafe sometimes felt that everyone belonged here except him—and now this girl, turning the air in the copying room blue. Her involuntary exclamation had been so unexpected that he had stopped as he walked past the door, captivated by the slight girl in a neat, dull suit swearing at the photocopier.

Entertained by the contrast, Rafe had been unable to resist finding out more.

He hadn't seen her before. At least, he didn't think so. The most memorable thing about her seemed to be the plain brown hair pulled tightly back from her face in a very unflattering style. Rafe's first impression had been one of primness, contrasting sharply with the words coming out of her mouth, but as she stood there and looked back at him with eyes that were clear and green and very direct she suddenly didn't seem so nondescript any more, and his interest sharpened.

'We haven't met, have we?'

'No,' she said curtly. 'I'm just a temp.'

'Well, welcome.' Apparently oblivious to her lack of enthusiasm, he smiled and held out his hand. 'I'm Rafe Knighton.'

As if she wasn't supposed to know!

Miranda might have little interest in celebrities, but even she knew about Rafe Knighton. He had been the ultimate playboy until four or five years ago when he had disappeared from London, presumably to drift around some other playground of the rich and famous, and there had been almost feverish excitement in the gossip pages when he had returned a couple of months earlier to take up the reins of the Knighton Group.

His father had famously keeled over with a heart attack in the middle of negotiating a mega-million dollar deal in New York and since then the business pages had been full of speculation about Rafe's ability to step into his father's spectacularly successful shoes.

Speculation of a more lurid nature was equally rife in the gossip columns and celebrity magazines. At thirty-five, Rafe was still unmarried, and since inheriting his father's fortune was rarely mentioned without the tag of 'the most eligible bachelor in Britain' attached to his name. He was welcomed back onto the A-list with open arms, and was photographed with any number of beautiful women on his arm, but as yet there had been no obvious front-runner for the title of Mrs Knighton.

Miranda knew all this because her younger sister, Octavia, avidly drank up every mention of Rafe Knighton and was determined to meet him. She had been delighted when she had heard that Miranda would be working for the Knighton Group.

'Wangle me an invitation to meet Rafe,' she had urged her sister, while Miranda had stared at her in disbelief.

'Octavia, I'm only there as a temp,' she tried to tell her. 'Temps don't even *see* chief executives, let alone meet them and get on wangling terms! They're right at the bottom of the pecking order. I won't even get within spitting distance of Rafe Knighton.'

And yet, here he was, holding out his hand, and clearly waiting for her to introduce herself.

Miranda sighed inwardly. She disapproved of everything Rafe Knighton stood for, and she didn't like the way he seemed to fill up the room with his good looks and his smile and that almost tangible charm. That feeling that he was using more than his fair share of the room left her edgy and more than a little breathless, and Miranda didn't like it at all, but she could hardly refuse to shake his hand.

'Miranda Fairchild,' she said reluctantly, and touched her palm to his.

She made to withdraw it right away, but Rafe was too quick for her. His fingers closed warm and firm around hers in a proper clasp as he smiled down at her. The touch of his hand sent a strange feeling snaking down her spine, and she snatched her hand away, prickling with irritation.

Couldn't he let up with that macho charm for an instant? It was so clearly an automatic reaction with him. All that intense gazing into her eyes and smiling and holding her hand just a little too long!

Miranda was exasperated. Surely he didn't expect her to believe that he had actually *seen* her? He was like a big tom cat on the prowl, making overtures to any female that happened to cross his path. Look at him, just waiting for her to melt at the knees and smile mistily back at him!

She had absolutely no intention of gratifying his vanity by smiling at all, let alone mistily, but she was annoyed to discover that her knees were not, in fact, quite as steady as they should have been.

Miranda scowled at the thought, and Rafe raised an eyebrow at her expression. 'Is there a problem?'

Perversely, this evidence that he was not only seeing her but watching her quite closely made Miranda even crosser. She could hardly tell him the truth: Oh, I'm just irritated with my knees for going all weak when you smiled. Now she was going to have to lie, and she hated doing that.

'I'm sorry, it's just a bit sore,' she improvised, holding up her grazed finger and taking the opportunity to step back. Why couldn't he go away and leave her alone?

'You've hurt yourself?' Rafe frowned in quick concern at the raw graze on her hand.

'*I* didn't do it,' she corrected him crisply. 'It was the photocopier that bit me. I told you it started it! I don't know why you're worrying about the machine. You should get in touch with the RSPCT instead.'

'The Royal Society for the Prevention of Cruelty to…?'

'Temps,' she said, and he laughed.

She reminded him of a little bird, he thought, one with drab plumage but bright-eyed and alert. Rafe liked people and usually people liked him back, but since he had taken over Knighton's he had come to wonder whether there was an element of sycophancy in the smiles that met him wherever he went. This girl with her prim outfit and her crisp voice and her clear, disapproving gaze made a refreshing change.

'That looks sore,' he said. 'Are you OK?'

'Don't worry, I'm not going to sue you for a grazed finger!' she said and turned back to the photocopier, but Rafe was intrigued now, and refused to take the hint that he should leave her to get on.

Instead he settled himself against the table and studied her with a discerning eye. It was a long time since he had met a woman who made so little of herself. That suit she was wearing was appalling, for instance. There was no way of telling what kind of figure she had, but she had other assets, Rafe realised on looking closer. Her hair was an ordinary brown, but shiny and very clean, and she had beautiful skin and quiet, fine-boned features. If she wore a better-fitting suit, let down her hair and bothered with a little make-up, she wouldn't look too bad at all.

'Which department are you working in?'

'Communications,' said Miranda briefly, wishing that he would go away. She crouched down and peered into the photocopier again.

'Ah, yes, you must be covering for Simon's PA... Is it Helen? Isn't there some problem with her mother?'

'It's Ellen, and it's her father who's ill,' Miranda corrected him, but she was secretly impressed that he had remembered as much as he had. In her experience as a temp, chief executives of companies the size of the Knighton Group rarely bothered to learn the names of their junior staff, let alone remember details of their domestic problems. 'I'm just covering for a week while she sorts out some care for him.'

'And after that?'

She shrugged. 'I'll have to hope the agency comes up with another assignment for me.'

'Have you been temping long?'

'A few months,' she said uninformatively.

Rafe looked down at her as she frowned into the photocopier. The overhead light gleamed on her hair, and his gaze noted the sweep of her lashes and the way the fine brows were drawn together over her nose. Her face had intelligence and character, he thought. She seemed an unlikely temp somehow.

'What were you doing before that?'

She shot an irritated glance up at him. 'Are you always this interested in your temporary staff?'

'I'm interested in all my staff,' said Rafe, wondering why she didn't want to tell him. 'How do you find Knighton's as a place to work?'

Miranda shrugged. 'It's fine. Everyone is very professional.'

Except the chief executive, she wanted to add, but didn't. Temping might be a bit of a climb-down from board member, but she needed the money and there were worse places for temporary placements.

Working here was bittersweet. So much was familiar. Like Fairchild's, the Knighton Group was a family business, a dynasty, but one that had embraced new technologies and business practices to become a household name with global interests, while Fairchild's had traded for too long on its past reputation.

Still, there was no use feeling bitter. She had a job to do, and she just wished Rafe Knighton would let her get on with it instead of lounging there interrogating her about things that were none of his business.

'It's just a shame about the machinery,' she added, pulling awkwardly at the toner cartridge, and muttering under her breath as it stuck firmly in place.

'Can I help?' asked Rafe, bending down to peer into the machine.

'Not unless you'd like to go out and buy a new photocopier,' said Miranda as crisply as she could, but it was hard with him so close beside her. The room was airless enough to begin with, and with six feet of male looming over her she was feeling distinctly short of oxygen.

'Is it broken?'

'I can't get the toner cartridge out.'

'I like to make sure my staff have the equipment they need

to do their jobs properly,' said Rafe, 'and I don't want you to think I'm mean, but purchasing an entirely new machine when we just need to replace a cartridge does seem a *touch* extravagant.'

Miranda sucked in her breath, irritated anew by the undercurrent of laughter in his voice. 'I wasn't being serious,' she snapped. Cautiously, she reached back into the innards of the copier. 'If I could just...' She grunted with effort, grimacing as her fingers felt for the catch once more. 'Oh, come *on*, stop being so difficult!'

Rafe observed her with amusement as she sat back on her heels with a sigh of frustration. 'Do you always talk to photocopiers?'

'I've got this theory they're like horses,' Miranda told him. 'When you're a temp, you spend a lot of time wrestling with photocopiers. They're always skittish at first, and they play up the moment they sense you don't know what you're doing. You have to get to know them every time, and let them know who's boss.'

'You mean you're a sort of office equipment whisperer?'

'Not a very effective one at the moment.'

Miranda sighed and gave up on the catch, but as she pulled her hand out, she caught her finger again. Same metal, same finger. 'Ow!' she said, shaking it. 'Maybe I am serious about you buying a new one!' she added to Rafe. 'I could take a hammer to this one first, and then you'd have to replace it.'

'Let me have a go.'

Rafe hitched up the trousers of his perfect Italian suit and crouched down beside her.

At close quarters, he was overwhelmingly male. Miranda scuttled crab-wise away from him as far as she could go, but there was very little room to manoeuvre between the table and the photocopier, and in the end she scrambled to her feet instead. At least that way she could breathe.

'I don't think that's a very good idea,' she said.

'Why not?'

'You're too well dressed,' she told him bluntly, trying to ignore the way every cell in her body still seemed to be humming with awareness of the leashed power beneath the suave exterior. 'Changing the toner cartridge can be a very messy business.'

'So can letting temps loose with hammers,' he said, glancing up at her with a grin that infuriatingly made Miranda's heart skip a beat.

Scowling at herself, she watched as Rafe put his hand into the copier, grasped the cartridge, and jerked it sharply forwards so that it shot out of its slot at last.

'There you go,' he said. He unclipped the used cartridge and lifted it out.

'Thank you,' said Miranda reluctantly.

'Don't mention it,' said Rafe. 'I don't often get the chance to make myself useful!'

She eyed him uncertainly, unsure if he was joking or not. On the whole, she thought not. He certainly didn't have the air of a man used to menial tasks, and why would he? Few people could have led such a pampered and privileged life as Rafe Knighton.

'Careful!' she warned as he straightened with the cartridge still in his hand. Bitter experience had taught her that used toner had a tendency to leak badly, and Rafe wouldn't be nearly so pleased with himself if he ended up with the fine black powder all over that immaculate suit. He looked the fastidious type, and she didn't have time to deal with an executive's wardrobe emergency this morning.

But it appeared that Rafe was more competent than he seemed. He set the cartridge down without so much as a particle of powder escaping. 'I'm not as careless as I look,' he told her, almost as if reading her mind, and then he smiled at her expression.

Miranda wished he would stop doing that. Her heart knocked into her ribs again, and, desperate to put a few more inches between them, she found herself backing into the table until it dug into the back of her thighs. She was grateful to him for fixing the copier, of course, but now he should just *go away*.

Close up, Rafe was less handsome than he seemed from a distance and in the glossy magazine photographs, she realised. It should have been reassuring, but the unevenness of his features and the faint prickle of stubble gave him a rough edge that paradoxically made the dark, glinting eyes and the mobile mouth more attractive rather than less, and all at once she was suffocatingly aware of him, of the clean, *expensive* smell of him, of the faint quiver of laughter she could sense vibrating beneath the suave exterior, of his massive, solid warmth so close to her.

Swallowing, Miranda turned away to busy herself inserting the new toner cartridge. Once it had clicked into place, she wiped around the copier to remove any spilt ink and closed the front of the machine with a snap.

'Now, get on with it!' she told it, relieving her feelings with a jab at the start button.

Obediently, the copier whirred into action.

'That's what I like to see,' said Rafe, who had been watching her with amusement. 'A firm hand! There's no mistaking who's boss around here, is there?'

'Very funny,' said Miranda mirthlessly, her eyes on the copies that were emerging from the machine. After all the hassle the copier had given her this morning, it was hard to believe that it was actually doing what it was supposed to do.

She couldn't believe Rafe had actually joked about who was in charge. He seemed to have no sense of his own importance. He was unlike any boss she'd ever encountered before. He definitely wasn't the kind of boss *she* had been in those last disastrous months at Fairchild's.

In her experience, bosses maintained their distance from the staff, either because they were too busy, or because they were concerned about their own status. They certainly didn't drift around the way Rafe Knighton evidently did. Miranda couldn't think of any other boss she had known who would hang around in the copying room, winding up the new temp or attempting to fix a photocopier themselves. Didn't he have anything better to do?

That unnerving awareness of him as a powerful male was fading, and she could dismiss him once more as little more than a clothes horse for expensive suits, an empty-headed celebrity wandering around his own company because he didn't know what to do with himself.

'Were you looking for anyone in particular?' she asked repressively.

'I was hoping to have a word with Simon,' said Rafe, recalled to a sense of his original purpose. 'Is he around?'

'He's out, I'm afraid. He'll be back this afternoon. He's got a meeting at two.' Miranda nodded at the papers stacking up in the copier tray. 'That's what all this copying is for.'

'I'll catch him later, then,' said Rafe easily.

'Shall I ask him to call you when he gets back?'

'You could do,' he said, 'or I'll wander down again a bit later. I only took over a month or so ago, and I'm still trying to get to know everybody,' he explained, seeing that Miranda was looking unimpressed by this casual approach. 'I like to walk round myself and see what's going on rather than wait for staff to come to me. That's how I get to know people like you and learn interesting things I didn't know, like rude words and how to talk to photocopiers!'

Miranda flushed slightly. Didn't he take anything seriously? 'Can I tell Simon what it's in connection with?' she asked, deliberately formal.

'I've got an idea I want to discuss with him,' said Rafe. 'I think we should hold a ball.'

A ball? Miranda's lips tightened disapprovingly. Rafe ought to be worrying about investment and product development and financial forecasts, not parties and balls and getting his photo in the papers! He reminded her all too bitterly of her father, who had been bored by the nitty gritty of business and had poured all his energy—not to mention the firm's profits—into putting on a show. Rafe Knighton had a reputation as a hell-raiser, and Miranda hoped that he wasn't going to throw away everything his father and grandfather had achieved the way her own father had done at Fairchild's.

'I'll tell Simon as soon as he gets back,' she said curtly as she collected the first set of copies and banged them lightly on the top of the machine to straighten them into a neat pile.

Rafe was left with the distinct feeling that he had been dismissed. For a moment he wavered between irritation and amusement—who did this temp think she was?—but, as so often with him, amusement won. He had to admire her gall, if nothing else.

'I'll leave you to it, then,' he said. 'Nice to meet you, Miranda Fairchild.'

Miranda watched him go, shaking her head slightly. Thank goodness he had gone, she thought. Perhaps now she could get on with some work. It had been impossible to concentrate with him looming over her, charging the air with his mere presence and making her nerves fizz and prickle. He would be much better off staying in his boardroom than wandering around unsettling people like that.

She slotted another set of papers into the feeder and pressed the copy button again.

It looked like being a long day, and she still had tonight to get through. When Rosie had asked her if she wanted to help out on occasional evenings waitressing, Miranda had jumped at the prospect of earning a bit of extra money, but it was hard work being on your feet all evening, and there were times, like now, when she wanted nothing so much as to go back to the flat and flop in front of the television all evening.

But it would be worth it when she had earned enough to move to Whitestones, Miranda thought fiercely, squaring her shoulders. Think about the house, she told herself. Think about the cliffs and the sound of the sea on the shingle.

Think about leaving London and the likes of Rafe Knighton far behind.

It would all be worth it then.

'You *cannot* be serious!'

Miranda held up the uniform Rosie had presented her and stared at it, aghast.

Rosie shifted uncomfortably. 'I know it's a bit tacky, but the organisers have insisted all the waiting staff wear these.'

'They want us to dress up as *cats*?'

'I think they thought it would be funny,' said Rosie with a sigh.

'Hilarious,' said Miranda acidly. She dropped the cat suit back on the pile with a gesture of distaste. 'What's wrong with a black skirt, a white blouse and a frilly pinny?'

'It's a book launch,' Rosie said miserably. 'One of those novelty self-help books, How to Unleash your Inner Pussy Cat or something like that. If you think the uniform is tasteless, you should see the goodie bag!'

'We don't really have to wear this, do we?' The skin-tight cat suit came complete with a fluffy tail and a cat mask with ears and whiskers. Miranda eyed it with dismay. 'Can't we just refuse?'

'Oh, please, Miranda!' Rosie begged. 'I wouldn't ask, but this is a really important contract for me. They've said if it goes well they'll offer me other jobs, and I think they have launches like this all the time. I can't afford to get their backs up by being difficult about everything. It all needs to go perfectly tonight.'

Miranda sighed. She knew how Rosie was struggling to get her new business off the ground. Rosie was a fantastic cook who made the kind of delicious, witty, and innovative canapés that were perfect for events catering, but so much business depended on establishing a reputation, and her friend badly needed a break.

How could Miranda let her down? Rosie had been her best friend since they were at school together. Other so-called friends had kept their distance, not wanting to be associated with dreary failure, when Fairchild's had collapsed and Miranda's world had come tumbling about her ears, but Rosie had stuck by her. She had a tiny flat at the very end of the Tube line, but had given Miranda a room without hesitation, asking well below the going rate for rent.

Temping by day, Miranda was glad to earn extra money in the evenings by helping Rosie out. Sometimes she just washed dishes or helped with the preparations, but for big events like this one she acted as waitress. Normally she wore black and blended into the background, but occasionally the client asked Rosie if the staff could wear something special. Tonight was the first time they had been presented at the last minute with quite such a ridiculous costume, but, looking at Rosie's anxious expression, Miranda knew that she couldn't refuse.

'Oh, all right,' she said, and watched her friend's face clear magically. 'It's not as if anyone is going to recognise me with that mask on! And who notices the waitresses anyway?'

Nobody might notice her, but it was hard not to feel very conspicuous indeed once she was squeezed into the cat suit. It clung to her figure in a way that was embarrassingly revealing.

'Actually, you look great,' said Rosie, surprised, when Miranda presented herself for duty. She walked round her, inspecting her critically. 'You've got a really good figure, Miranda, but you keep it hidden away beneath those shapeless jackets you wear.'

'I could do with a shapeless jacket now,' sighed Miranda, plucking fretfully at the suit. 'I might as well be naked!'

'It's not that bad,' Rosie consoled her. 'When you've got your mask on you won't feel so exposed.'

Miranda wasn't sure about that, but it was too late to back out now. Nobody ever noticed her, anyhow, so why should tonight be any different?

The mask made her feel a little more confident, but she was still very conscious of the stares that seemed to follow her as she threaded her way through the crowd with a tray, and she was dismayed to spot Octavia on the far side of the room. Looking as beautiful as ever, her little sister was flirting with a soap star who was rumoured to be about to hit the big time, and leave his second wife in the process.

Miranda found it hard to shake the habit of worrying about Octavia, but she was fairly sure that her sister would just be amusing herself. For a girl who looked the way she did, Octavia was surprisingly hard-headed when it came to men. Still, she had better avoid that side of the room, Miranda decided. She wouldn't put it past Octavia to recognise her, mask or no mask, and she and Belinda complained enough about her evening job as it was.

'It's so shaming,' they grumbled. 'What if anyone recognises you as our sister?' Personally, Miranda felt it was more shaming to sponge off friends the way Octavia did, or depend financially on your in-laws as Belinda clearly had to do, but she had given up arguing with her sisters years ago.

Wheeling round, she headed the other way, and wound her way through the crowd, tray balanced aloft and tail draped over one arm to stop herself tripping over it. Champagne was circulating freely and the party soon warmed up, the chatter getting louder, the laughter more raucous.

Miranda's feet were aching as she refilled the tray with exquisite little mushroom vol-au-vents and smoked salmon and scrambled egg canapés and headed back into the party once more.

There was Octavia again, sparkling up at a portly businessman. Miranda veered away and headed instead towards a group standing at the edge of the room. An incredibly slender girl wearing a dramatic dress that had probably cost as much as Miranda would earn in a year was looking bored, and as she got closer Miranda could guess why. The men with her had all obviously imbibed freely and were laughing uproariously at each other's jokes.

Miranda wondered why the girl bothered to stay since she was so clearly unamused. She was standing close to a tall man with his back to Miranda, a possessive hand on his arm. Perhaps she would rather be bored than give up her position at his side?

He must be quite something, thought Miranda cynically. A girl like that wouldn't bother unless he was very rich, very famous or very gorgeous, and she was clearly ready to defend her territory against the likes of Octavia. Needless to say, she didn't even notice Miranda, proffering her tray, but her companion turned to look at her, and Miranda stopped dead, her heart lurching into her throat and wiping the smile from her face.

Now she could see why the girl was prepared to endure tedious jokes rather than abandon him—he was indeed very rich, very famous *and* very gorgeous, loath as Miranda was to admit it.

Rafe Knighton, in fact.

CHAPTER TWO

RAFE was looking straight at Miranda and the directness of his gaze made her burningly aware once more of her revealing costume. For one wild moment she was tempted to turn tail and run.

Then she told herself not to be so silly. Even if Rafe were to remember her from earlier that day, which was frankly pretty unlikely, there was no way he could recognise the sexily clad 'cat' as the colourless temp at the photocopier.

She forced a smile and held out the tray instead. 'Would you like anything?'

The girl flicked a dismissive glance over her and looked away, not even bothering with a refusal, but the other men leered openly.

'I know what I'd like,' said one to a burst of laughter, 'and it's not on the tray!'

'Here, pussy, pussy,' called another in a high, stupid voice. 'I'd like a stroke.'

Rafe was not enjoying himself. Why did he bother to come to these events? He had hoped to meet a rather more serious crowd at a book launch, but he should have known better. This party was even sillier than usual, and whose tasteless idea had it been to dress the waitresses as cats? They were all obviously hating it.

It was depressing to realise that someone had thought he would belong at a party like this. Had he really used to feel part of this life? Rafe was beginning to despair of ever persuading anyone that he had changed and was no longer the spoiled trust-fund baby that temp this morning had so obviously thought he was. No one was interested in what he had been doing for the past four years. No one was interested in what he was doing now. They all just assumed that he was playing at running the Knighton Group, and that the real decisions were being made by the board of directors.

About to feel sorry for himself, Rafe looked at the waitress, her smile rigidly in place. Poor girl. There were worse fates than inheriting a blue chip company, after all. He could be the one wearing the stupid costume and trying to earn a living while everyone else drank champagne and made lewd suggestions at his expense.

'I'll have one, thanks,' he said, interrupting the increasingly risqué comments in an attempt to distract his companions, and she stepped forward gratefully with the tray.

As she did so the man standing next to her decided to put his words into action and patted her bottom, and Rafe saw her jerk unthinkingly away from his touch. He didn't blame her for that at all, but the sudden movement tilted the tray, sending a selection of canapés shooting forward to land in a smear of pastry, egg and mushroom sauce all down the front of his jacket.

There was a moment of appalled silence.

Kyra was the first to speak. 'You stupid girl!' she snapped. 'His jacket's ruined.'

'It wasn't her fault,' said Rafe sharply. He looked at the waitress, who was staring, aghast, at his jacket. 'Are you OK?'

'I'm *so* sorry,' she said. Crouching down, she began hastily gathering the mess onto her tray while Kyra rolled her eyes and looked pointedly away, and the men shifted quickly into a new grouping, turning their backs on the whole sorry mess.

Rafe bent to help her. 'It's not you that should be sorry,' he pointed out. 'You shouldn't have to put up with hassle like that.'

'These outfits are asking for trouble,' she said philosophically. 'I shouldn't have jumped like that, but he took me by surprise. I'm not used to anyone noticing me.'

She sounded quite sincere, Rafe realised to his surprise. He would have imagined that a girl with that figure would be fighting men off all the time. True, he couldn't see much of her face, but she had beautiful skin, and, although what little he could see of her expression was rather ironic, those legs were spectacular. He was having trouble keeping his eyes off them, in fact, even if it did make him feel a creep, and not much better than the guy who had groped her.

'Thank you for your help,' she said briskly as she straightened. 'And thank you for not making a fuss. My friend is responsible for the catering, and this is her first big job. I don't want to cause any trouble for her.'

'Don't worry about it,' Rafe said, picking a piece of scrambled egg off his tie, and wondering why she suddenly seemed oddly familiar.

'Here,' she said helpfully, shifting the tray onto the crook of her arm so she could pick up the fluffy tail and use the end to brush the last of the crumbs from his front.

'At least this stupid tail is useful for *something*,' she said.

There it was again, that peculiar conviction that he had met her before somewhere. Rafe frowned slightly. Surely he wouldn't have forgotten those legs?

'I'm so sorry,' she said, misinterpreting his frown. 'There are still some marks on your suit. I should pay your dry-cleaning bill.'

'Forget it,' said Rafe easily. He was naturally neat, and there had been a time when he would have been bothered by a less than immaculate appearance, but the last four years had taught him that there were more important things than the odd stain. He certainly wasn't going to accept what he suspected were the hard-won wages of a cocktail waitress. It hadn't even been her fault.

'It was high time this suit was cleaned anyway,' he went on, when she hesitated. 'You've done me a favour, really. Now I'll have to do something about it.'

Behind her mask, Miranda regarded him in some puzzlement. Could it be that appearances were deceptive, after all? He had that glossy, well groomed look that was usually accompanied by an obsession with appearance, and she had expected him to make a huge fuss about the mess she had made of his jacket. Instead of which, he had been really very nice about it all. Few of the other guests at this party would have bothered to help out a frazzled waitress, that was for sure.

Miranda almost wished that he hadn't. It was never comfortable having one's preconceptions challenged, and she didn't really want to think that there might be more to Rafe Knighton than met the eye.

The girl beside him hadn't even made a token effort to help, but now that the mess was cleared up she was homing back in on Rafe. Miranda was amused to see the way she stepped slightly between them, turning her back to edge Miranda away. Not that she needed to worry, Miranda thought. She had absolutely no interest in the Rafe Knightons of this world. She knew only too well what it was like to live with a playboy.

You'd have thought that growing up with a father like theirs would have put her sisters off the idea of marrying anyone like him, but apparently not. Miranda couldn't understand why Belinda had been so determined to marry a title, while Octavia, more practical, had set her sights on a wealthy husband. Their own parents had had the society wedding of the year in their day, and look how badly that marriage had turned out!

As if her thoughts had conjured her sister up, Miranda caught sight of Octavia somewhere behind Rafe's shoulder. She was casually scanning the crowd, but as Miranda watched the beautiful green eyes widened as they fell upon Rafe's profile.

Time to beat a retreat, Miranda decided. If she knew her sister, Octavia would be over here any moment now to introduce herself, and she didn't want to be here when she did. Not that she cared about embarrassing Octavia, but it would be awkward if her sister somehow revealed her identity to Rafe. She would just as soon not be exposed to her boss while she was wearing a skin-tight cat suit.

'I'd better go and get rid of this mess,' she said to Rafe, backing away to his girlfriend's evident relief. 'Sorry again about your jacket.'

Rafe watched her slip away through the crowd. She had a very straight back, and he was conscious of the same odd feeling of knowing her somehow. His brows drew together in an effort to focus his memory. Where could he possibly have seen her before?

Beside him, he was vaguely aware of Kyra stiffening. 'I'm bored with this party,' she said abruptly, taking his arm with a proprietorial air. 'Let's go.'

Rafe hesitated. Kyra had attached herself to him early in the evening and he had been wondering how to shake her off without hurting her feelings. He had no intention of spending the rest of the night with her, but nor did he want to stay at this stupid party just to make a point. They could leave together and then go their separate ways, he decided.

As they turned to go he literally bumped into an enchantingly pretty girl, but Kyra towed him onwards before they had chance to do more than exchange apologetic smiles. Rafe glanced back over his shoulder with a faint frown as he left. There had been something elusively familiar about her too.

The thought made him pause at the door and look around to see if he could spot the waitress again, but there were too many people.

'Come on,' said Kyra impatiently, and, stifling an odd pang of disappointment, Rafe went.

'Hiya.'

Startled, Miranda looked up from her computer to see her youngest sister lounging in the doorway, and as usual making it appear that the door had been specifically designed to show her off to her best advantage.

'Octavia! You're not supposed to be in here. There are supposed to be security procedures to stop strangers getting in!'

Security at the Knighton Group was run by a gimlet-eyed ex-Army officer called Mack who took his responsibilities extremely seriously. Miranda sometimes thought it would be easier to stroll into Fort Knox with a handy bag for carrying bullion.

'Oh, it's OK,' said Octavia carelessly, strolling into the office and looking around her with a kind of bemused curiosity. This was a place where people actually *worked*. 'I spoke to someone called Mack—he's sweet, isn't he?—and told him it was an emergency, so he said it would be fine if I just came up. He told me where to find your office and everything.'

Miranda stiffened. 'Emergency? What's wrong?'

'Nothing, I just wanted to see you, and I knew I'd never get near you unless I said it was important.' Octavia spun a chair from the other desk and sat down on it, crossing her impossibly long legs. 'You'd just say you were busy or something.'

'I *am* busy,' said Miranda, eyeing her sister with exasperation. Honestly, Octavia was impossible sometimes! 'So why don't you just tell me what you're doing here?'

Octavia leant forward. 'I was *this* close to meeting Rafe Knighton last night,' she said, holding her thumb and forefinger together to demonstrate the nearness by which she had missed Rafe. 'But he was with that cow Kyra Bennett, who saw me coming and whisked him away before I could introduce myself. I smiled and Rafe definitely looked interested.' She pouted. 'I just *know* he would have wanted to talk to me if she hadn't been dragging him off.'

'And I'm interested in all this because…?'

'Because now I just need another chance to bump into him,' said Octavia, ignoring Miranda's sardonic expression. 'I'm sure he'd recognise me, and I can take it from there.'

Miranda sighed. 'Take what from where?' she asked, knowing that she probably wasn't going to like the answer.

She didn't.

'Things are desperate,' announced Octavia. 'I don't like not having any money,' she said simply. 'It's been horrid with Daddy dying and not having any money any more. I don't even get an allowance now!' The green eyes were wide with indignation. 'My only option is to marry someone rich, and Rafe Knighton is as rich as they come. He's rather gorgeous too, don't you think? I wouldn't mind sacrificing myself to him!'

'That's very noble of you, Octavia, but I do have to point out that marriage is not, in fact, your only option,' said Miranda crisply. 'You could always try working for a living like the rest of us.'

'Why would I want to do that if I could get married instead and never have to work at all?' Octavia countered, all reasonableness. 'You wouldn't have to either if I was Mrs Knighton. Octavia Knighton…' She tried out the name musingly. 'It's got a nice ring to it, don't you think?'

Miranda put her head in her hands. Sometimes she despaired of her sisters. They seemed to live in a parallel universe, one at least two centuries behind the times to boot.

'And all *you've* got to do is introduce me to your boss,' Octavia pointed out. 'Is that too much to ask? What's the problem?'

Where to start? Sighing, Miranda lifted her head.

'One, I'm completely opposed on principle to the idea of

marriage as a meal ticket,' she said, ticking off objections on her fingers. 'Two, even if I wasn't, Rafe Knighton would make the worst possible husband for you. He's just a pretty face with too much money, and he'd make you absolutely miserable.

'And *three*,' she finished with emphasis before she let herself remember that only the night before she had wondered if there might be rather more to Rafe than his looks, 'I don't have anything to do with him, so couldn't introduce you anyway. In case you've forgotten, I'm just a temp here. He's Chairman and Chief Executive. He never comes down here and if he did, he wouldn't even know who I was.'

The words were barely out of her mouth when Rafe walked into the office.

'Hello, Miranda,' he said.

For one dizzying moment, Miranda had the strangest feeling that all the oxygen had been sucked out of the room.

She had forgotten how *physical* he was. It had been a shock seeing him last night, but she had just managed to convince herself that he couldn't possibly be as good-looking as she remembered, and now here he was, looking more so, not less, in yet another immaculately stylish suit, exuding charm and confidence and an almost electrifying energy.

His presence was overwhelming, almost suffocating, and after that first breathless moment when Miranda hadn't been able to think at all her hackles rose instinctively. Really, he was too much. He was just too…too…too *everything*.

The last time she had seen him, she might as well have been naked. Miranda was mortified at the memory. He didn't realise it, of course—thank goodness she had been wearing a mask!— but it still made her uncomfortable to think about how provocative that stupid costume had been.

Not that Rafe had leered like the other men, she had to give him credit for that, but how typical of him to have been at such a mindless party in the first place, and with that vapid girl clinging to his arm.

Burningly aware of Octavia's accusing gaze, and offering up silent thanks to whoever had insisted the waitresses wore masks the night before, Miranda found a cool smile.

'What can I do for you, Mr Knighton?'

'You can call me Rafe, for a start,' said Rafe, disconcerted by how familiar she seemed, sitting prim and proper behind her desk in a suit that was, if anything, less flattering than the day before. The woman had no idea how to dress. 'Is Simon around? I never managed to talk to him about the ball yesterday.'

'A ball! How exciting!' A voice from the corner made Rafe turn and he found himself looking at a girl who might have been designed as a contrast to Miranda with her tight lips and her prudish expression.

She really was extraordinarily lovely, with flawless features and amazing green eyes. Silver gilt hair tumbled art-lessly to her shoulders, and a breathtakingly short skirt revealed incredible legs—quite as good as that waitress's last night—which she crossed as she leant forward with a dazzling smile.

'Hello!' she said as if she knew him.

'Hello.' He smiled back at her, and held out his hand. Unlike Miranda Fairchild, she looked as if she would enjoy a ball. She might be just the assistant he needed. 'I'm sorry, I didn't see you there before. I'm Rafe Knighton. Are you temping here, too?'

'Just visiting, I'm afraid.' Her eyes laughed up at him as she shook his hand. 'I'm Octavia Fairchild.'

Fairchild? 'You're Miranda's sister?' Rafe asked, unable to keep the surprise from his voice. It was hard to imagine two women more different from each other, one all lush, blonde beauty and the other prim and prickly and if not exactly plain, certainly nowhere near as lovely as her sister. Still, that explained why there was something familiar about her.

Octavia's green eyes flickered slightly. She wasn't used to being described as Miranda's sister. It was usually the other way round.

She kept her smile dazzling, though, and nodded. 'I know I shouldn't be here,' she confided, with a devastating glance up under her lashes, 'but I wanted to see how Miranda was getting on.'

'And discovered that I'm very busy,' Miranda finished crisply for her with a meaningful look that Octavia ignored entirely. 'Octavia's just leaving.'

'Don't let me chase you away,' said Rafe instantly. 'I just came to have a word with Simon.'

'He's in his office if you want to go in,' said Miranda, wishing he and Octavia would both go away, but before he could move the inner door opened and Simon himself came out.

'Miranda, could you—?' he began, then stopped as he saw Rafe. 'I didn't know you were here, Rafe,' he apologised. 'Have you been waiting long?'

'Not at all. I've just been meeting Miranda's sister here,' said Rafe easily, indicating Octavia.

To Miranda's surprise, Simon's expression was disapproving as it rested on her sister. He nodded a curt greeting and turned immediately back to Rafe. 'Come in,' he said, and gestured towards his office. 'What can I do for you?'

'Well!' Octavia was distinctly put out. '*He's* not very friendly, is he?'

'Actually, he's very nice,' said Miranda.

'You can keep him.' Octavia tossed back her hair with a sniff. 'I'd rather have Rafe any day. He's gorgeous, isn't he?'

'And no one knows it more than him,' Miranda pointed out.

'I think he liked me, don't you?'

Miranda didn't bother to answer that. Of course Rafe had liked Octavia. Men—with the apparent exception of Simon—always did.

She turned back to her computer. 'Octavia, I've got to get on.'

'I'll leave you to it, then,' said Octavia, getting gracefully to her feet. 'I don't want to look too keen. But if Rafe asks for my phone number, be sure and give it to him.'

Waggling her fingers in farewell, she strolled off, leaving Miranda alone with the scent of her perfume drifting in the air.

With a sigh, Miranda went back to her email.

It was nearly half an hour before Rafe emerged from Simon's office. Miranda was alert to the sound of the opening door, and this time she was braced against the good looks and the dark-eyed charm. Less easy to ignore was the way his presence sent a charge zapping and crackling through the air and interfering with her breathing no matter how desperately she kept her eyes firmly fixed on her computer screen and pretended to be absorbed.

'Have you got a moment, Miranda?' said Simon, and, because it was him, she looked up. 'Rafe has a proposal for you.'

Miranda looked wary. 'What sort of proposal?'

'Don't worry, I'm not going down on one knee,' said Rafe, with one of those smiles calculated to set a female pulse racing. Miranda kept hers below a gallop, but it was an effort. 'This proposal's to do with work, but I think it will be fun too.'

'Fun?'

Just as he'd thought, she sounded as if she didn't know what the word meant.

'I want you to work with me on a special assignment,' he told her. 'Organising a ball, in fact.'

Most girls would have been thrilled at the idea. Rafe was pretty sure her beautiful sister would have been, but Miranda just looked at Simon.

He beamed back at her, oblivious to her dismay. 'It's a great opportunity,' he said. 'I'm sure you'll be fantastic at it. I've just been telling Rafe how impressed we've all been by you.'

'But…won't you need me here?' she asked, trying to keep the desperation from her voice.

'Ellen will be back on Monday,' Simon pointed out. 'We'll miss you, of course, but it's great to know that you'll still be around for a while. We'll clear it with your agency, of course, but I'm sure they'll be delighted to let you stay when they hear what a prestigious assignment it is.'

Miranda was sure they would be too. Her heart sank, and she glanced at Rafe, who was watching her with evident amusement, as if he knew exactly how reluctant she was to take the job.

It wasn't the job that made her uneasy, it was *him*. He was too disturbing, too overwhelming. It was impossible to concentrate when he was around, making the atmosphere zing just by standing there, letting the corner of his mouth curl in a way that made it hard to breathe properly. She would never get any work done.

And even if she did manage to deal with those distractions, she would never be able to keep Octavia away once she found out what she was doing. Miranda had no intention of encouraging Octavia's dreams of becoming Mrs Knighton. There was no way coming up smack against a man as superficial and self-absorbed as herself would make her lovely sister happy. She needed to be cherished for her beauty and charm, not broken on the wheel of Rafe's 'fun' lifestyle.

But what could she say? She could hardly say that she didn't like him, or thought that the whole idea of a ball was typically frivolous and silly. A ball, in the twenty-first century! Honestly!

She lifted her chin. 'How long would this assignment last?'

'That depends on when the ball is,' said Rafe cheerfully. 'Your first task will be to set a date. But let's say a couple of months.'

'You'll never find a venue in that time.' Miranda seized on

the excuse. 'Anywhere big enough to a hold a ball will be booked up years in advance.'

'I've got an idea about that,' said Rafe, looking directly into her eyes. 'But before we talk about details, I need to know if you're available, and if you're willing to do the job.'

All she had to do was say that she had other commitments. She didn't have to do any job if she didn't want to.

But she needed the money, and there was no guarantee the agency would be able to find her another placement next week. Especially if she had turned down a plum assignment for no reason other than feeling unsettled by her prospective boss.

Don't be so silly, Miranda told herself sternly. The hard truth was that she needed the money, and two months of regular income would make a big difference. If she carried on working in the evenings as well, she could even start to save.

She thought about Whitestones and how much it was going to take to make the house habitable. Then she thought about the sea and the smell of the air and how happy she always felt there. It would be worth putting up with Rafe Knighton for that, wouldn't it?

And perhaps she wouldn't have to have that much to do with him after all, she encouraged herself. A man like him wasn't likely to involve himself in boring practicalities. She might never see him.

Taking a deep breath, Miranda looked steadily back into Rafe's eyes.

'I'm available,' she said, 'and I'm willing.'

On Monday morning, Miranda presented herself in the chief executive's office at nine o'clock on the dot. She was wearing a grey suit with a neat white blouse, and sensible black court shoes. She looked, she felt, cool and professional, and that was what she was determined to be.

Miranda had had the weekend to think about it, and she had decided that she had been overreacting to Rafe Knighton's unsettling presence. She had nearly refused this job because of him. How stupid would that have been?

It was humiliating to think that she had been rattled by glinting eyes and a wicked smile. Miranda squirmed whenever she remembered the way her pulse had jumped and jittered. She ought to be immune to his particular brand of good looks and charm, after all.

And she *was*, Miranda resolved. She was lucky to have a job at all, let alone the prospect of an interesting one. She was good at organising. A ball was a project like any other, and she was fairly sure Rafe Knighton would lose interest as soon as they got down to the tedious details. He would drift off to another idea, and she would be able to get on with the job.

It would be fine.

Rafe's PA, an elegant woman called Ginny, was clearly expecting her and made her welcome. She had even cleared a desk for her, but before Miranda had a chance to pump her about exactly what she was expected to do Rafe himself breezed into the office.

It was extraordinary the way everything snapped into focus when he was in the room, Miranda thought, conscious of a hitch in her breathing in spite of all her sternest resolutions not to notice him at all. She hadn't even been aware of how muted things had seemed until he appeared.

In place of his usual immaculate suit, he wore black jeans and an open-necked pink shirt, its sleeves rolled casually above broad, strong wrists. The colour should have made him look effeminate, but instead only emphasised the virile masculinity he managed to exude just standing there, and Miranda made herself look away while she concentrated on breathing steadily. Cool and professional, right?

Right.

Rafe was kissing Ginny on the cheek and teasing her about her weekend. His charm was relentless, Miranda thought, glad to be back in critical mode, encompassing everyone and everything in his path. She imagined it steamrollering over man, woman, child or dog, regardless of whether they wanted to be charmed or not. Was she the only one able to resist it?

Her father had been exactly the same. When he'd died, Miranda had lost count of the people who had told her that he was the most charming person they had ever met, but she had often wondered whether that expansive charm hid a desperate need for approval. It had always seemed to her that her father didn't exist properly unless he had someone to amuse or impress or flatter with his attention.

Rafe Knighton came from the same mould, Miranda suspected, and she would do well not to forget it.

'I'm glad to see you, Miranda,' said Rafe, turning his attention to her at last. 'And bang on time, too. I hope this means you're keen to get going on the ball?' His voice was warm with laughter and his eyes danced distractingly as they studied her, standing neat and composed by the desk.

What was so funny? Miranda thought crossly even as she reminded herself not to let him rile her. Lifting her chin, she returned his gaze levelly.

'It means I believe punctuality is important,' she said.

'What about at the end of the day? Are you one of those clock-watchers who'll drop everything and walk out at five-thirty, regardless of what needs to be done?'

Privately, Miranda thought Rafe Knighton was a fine one to talk about clock-watching when he had barely done a stroke of work in his life. Easy to sneer at people who were paid by the hour when you could drift around amusing yourself all day.

'No,' she said coolly. 'If anything needs to be dealt with

urgently, then of course I will stay—and include any extra hours on my timesheet,' she added, just in case he expected her to work for free.

'Excellent,' said Rafe. 'In that case, let's go.'

'Go?' Miranda stared at him. 'Go where?'

'I want you to see the ballroom I've got in mind and tell me what you think. You can't start organising the ball until you know where it's going to be.'

'Rafe, you can't drag the poor girl off before she's even had a chance to sit down!' Ginny protested.

'Poor girl? *Poor girl?*' Rafe shook his head. 'Don't let that demure look fool you, Ginny. Miranda isn't a poor girl. The entire communications department was terrified of her efficiency, and I've seen her beat their photocopier into submission with my own eyes! I won't tell you how she did it or what kind of language she used. You would be shocked!'

Out of the corner of his eye he saw Miranda's mouth twitch and, although she quickly suppressed her smile, he was conscious of a spurt of triumph at having got through to her at last. It was a relief to see that glimpse of humour, too. Perhaps he hadn't made such a colossal mistake after all.

He had been dismayed when he'd first walked in that morning to see her looking prim and proper in that dull suit and far more colourless than he had remembered. This ball was important, and if it was going to be a success it would have to be run by someone who had some sense of humour as well as excellent organisational abilities.

Rafe had liked Miranda's astringency when he had met her the week before, and that combined with the glowing references Simon had given her had made her seem like the perfect candidate. This morning, though, he had begun to wonder if the sharp Miranda he remembered had been a mere figment of his imagination. Now, seeing the curl at the corner of her mouth, he was reassured. She might not want to let on that she was amused by his nonsense, but Rafe knew better.

'At least have a cup of coffee first,' Ginny was urging, but now that he was sure Miranda was the girl he had remembered he was impatient to be off.

'You don't want coffee, do you, Miranda? I bet you don't even touch the stuff.'

'On the contrary,' she said. 'I depend on coffee to get me through the morning.'

Her eyes met his blandly, and meeting that clear green gaze, Rafe felt his pulse kick unexpectedly.

'We'll stop on the way,' he promised, turning back to Ginny. 'There's nothing that won't keep until tomorrow, is there?'

'Tomorrow?' Miranda repeated as she followed him out of the office. 'How long are we going to *be?'*

'We'll be away most of the day,' said Rafe casually. Pushing the button to call the express lift, he caught her look of dismay. 'Why, do you have to be back for a certain time?'

'Well, no...' she admitted. She had worked every evening over the weekend and was looking forward to a night in.

'Good. I hate having to be somewhere at a set time, don't you?'

'No,' said Miranda as the lift doors slid open and they stepped inside. 'I prefer to have a plan.'

Rafe glanced at her. As before, her hair was pulled tightly back from her face. A practical style, maybe, but not a flattering one, even if it did expose the pure line of her jaw and the chin tilted at what he suspected was a characteristically determined angle.

Her lips were pressed together in a tight line and she kept her eyes firmly fixed on the lights above the door. In that suit she looked neat and tense and far too controlled for comfort.

'Don't you ever feel like being spontaneous?' he asked.

The lift sighed to a halt on the ground floor and the doors

opened once more. 'I grew up in a family of spontaneous people,' said Miranda. 'In my experience, nothing ever happens unless you plan it.'

'There's nothing wrong with a bit of organisation,' Rafe agreed, holding open the door for her, 'but if you plan too much it takes away all the fun. Take today,' he went on as they stepped out into the spring sunshine. He gestured around. 'It's a beautiful day. If we had planned meetings we'd end up sitting in an office all day. As it is, we can do whatever we like with it.'

'You may be able to, but I can't afford to do that,' she pointed out crisply. 'I'm being paid to do whatever *you* want to do. If not, I wouldn't be here.'

'Where *would* you be? If you could do whatever you liked today?'

That was easy. Miranda thought of Whitestones on a day like today. The house would be full of sunshine, and at the bottom of the cliff the sea would be a-glitter in the bright light. 'I'd be at the seaside,' she said.

CHAPTER THREE

A GLEAMING convertible sports car was waiting at the bottom of the steps, engine idling, its soft top invitingly open. The moment Rafe appeared, the driver got out and handed him the keys before opening the passenger door for Miranda.

As she got in with a murmur of thanks Miranda thought about her trip to work that morning. She had had to walk to the Tube, then wait for a train. Engineering works had caused delays all along the line, and by the time she had eventually managed to squeeze onto a train she had had to spend the entire journey pressed up against all the other blank-faced, Monday-morning commuters.

Now, barely an hour later, transport had been brought to the door so that all she had to do was sink into the soft leather seat. The contrast was disorientating.

Rafe had finished exchanging racing tips with the driver and got in beside her. He smiled at her as he pulled on his seat belt and started the car.

'Which sea?'

Miranda blinked. 'Sorry?'

'You said that if you had a choice you'd be at the seaside. I wondered which coast you were thinking of.'

'Oh. The south coast,' she told him, watching as he pulled expertly out into the traffic. 'In Dorset.'

Her eyes took on a faraway expression as she pictured Whitestones. 'There's a house on a cliff, and steps that lead down to a shingle beach.' She sighed a little, remembering. 'I love it there.'

'Then we'll go.'

There was a strange note to Rafe's voice, and Miranda turned to stare at him. 'I thought we were going to look at a ballroom?'

'We are. We're going to have lunch with my grandmother who lives in Hampshire, but after that we'll drive on and find your beach.' He slanted her one of his smiles. 'There you are, we've got a plan after all.'

'You're not serious!'

'Of course I'm serious. I'm always serious,' said Rafe, but the navy blue eyes glinted in a very unserious way.

'We're going to Hampshire? For *lunch*?'

'And to see a ballroom. Don't forget this is work,' he said with mock reproof.

'But...does your grandmother have a ballroom?' This was turning into such a strange Monday morning that Miranda was beginning to find it all surreal.

'Indeed she does,' said Rafe cheerfully. 'Knighton Park is a monstrosity built by my great-great grandfather when he made his fortune. He was a typical bad boy made good, and once he'd made some money he was determined to flaunt it. He built a pile that everyone else must have thought was impossibly vulgar, with every mod con of the time...including a ballroom that's hardly been used since. My grandmother has lived there since she was married.'

'I thought the ball would be in London,' said Miranda, frowning slightly.

'That would be ideal, but, as you pointed out, we're unlikely to find anywhere if we don't want to wait until next year now...and I don't.'

No, Rafe would never want to wait for anything. He was a typical trust fund baby, expecting that he could have whatever he wanted, whenever he wanted it, thought Miranda, conveniently forgetting that she had grown up in a family that acted on very similar assumptions.

'What's the big hurry?'

The traffic lights chose that moment to turn red, and Rafe pulled up with a little sigh of frustration. Yanking on the handbrake with unnecessary force, he turned to look at Miranda, sitting straight-backed beside him. 'Don't you ever wake up with an idea and want to make it happen straight away?'

'If it's a good idea, it's worth taking the time to make sure it happens right,' she said, thinking of Whitestones. 'We can't always snap our fingers and have exactly what we want immediately,' she added reprovingly.

'No, but if we don't at least try to make it happen, we may never have what we want,' Rafe pointed out. He might have known she wouldn't understand. Look at her, buttoned up so tightly it was surprising she could breathe! She didn't look as if she had ever done anything spontaneous in her life. On the other hand, the seaside had been an interesting choice. He'd have expected her to opt for something dull, like a library or a museum.

'Maybe you're right,' he said, his eyes on the lights and his foot on the clutch, ready for the off. 'Maybe it would be best to leave it for another year, but if there's any chance of arranging something for this summer, I want to make it happen.

'See what you think about the ballroom at Knighton Park,' he went on, enjoying the sense of leashed power as the engine revved. 'It's not that far from London. It might work. If you don't think it will, OK. We can look around for a venue for next year, at which point you'll have organised your way out of a job, but in the meantime we may as well make the most of a day out, don't you think? You're getting paid for it, after all.'

Miranda felt the pressure against the small of her back as the lights changed to green and the car accelerated away. They were heading down Park Lane. On their right, Hyde Park looked bright and inviting, with the trees decked out in fresh green. It had been a long, grey winter and an even greyer spring, and now London was unfurling in the sunshine.

This was not the Monday morning she had expected, cocooned in the comfort of a luxurious car, driving out of town for lunch in the country and, as Rafe pointed out, getting paid for it. She didn't often get a day off, so she might as well make the most of it, just as he'd suggested. Settling back into the leather, Miranda tipped her face to the sunshine, closed her eyes and smiled.

Rafe nearly went off the road. He had been aware of that rigidly prim pose slowly relaxing, and, glancing sideways, was struck afresh by the beautiful skin and the fine brows, by the clean lines of her face and throat. Last week, her hair had seemed dull and brown and straight, but the sunlight turned it to myriad shades of gold and honey, and made him wonder what it would be like if she let it fall around her face, whether it would feel as smooth and silky as it looked if he tangled his fingers in it.

And then she had smiled. She wasn't even smiling at him. It was just a smile of sheer pleasure in the moment, but Rafe was startled. It was as if he had lifted a curtain, expecting to see a plain, ordinary girl behind it, and instead found himself staring at a lush, sensuous woman.

Had her mouth always been that wide? That sensual? Had it always curled in that tantalising way?

Thrown, Rafe gripped the steering wheel and concentrated fiercely on the traffic. Who would have thought that prim Miranda Fairchild would have a smile like that? And if that was how she smiled at the feel of sunshine on her face, how would she smile if she were happy? In love?

In bed?

Rafe dragged his mind away from the image with difficulty. He was more shaken than he wanted to admit by that brief glimpse of a different side to Miranda Fairchild. He wished he hadn't seen that smile. He didn't want her to be attractive and distracting. Although he hadn't put it into words, he had decided that she would be ideal for this job precisely because he had thought she was neither. She was supposed to be intelligent and practical and unassuming, and nothing else. She wasn't supposed to *smile*.

Not like that anyway.

'Dreaming you're back at the photocopier?' he asked, keeping his voice determinedly light.

To his relief, Miranda laughed and opened her eyes. 'No, I'm not missing that copier at all.' Straightening, she looked around her. 'It's not a *bad* way to spend a Monday morning, I suppose! This reminds me of when my father used to drive me down to see my godmother in Dorset. He had an open-topped sports car, too.'

How long was it since she had thought about that? Miranda wondered a little guiltily. She ought to remember the good times with her father more often. Much better to remember him when he was the golden, carefree father she had idolised, than to think about the foolish vanity and obstinacy that had brought the entire family to ruin.

She pushed the dark thoughts determinedly aside. 'It's hard to believe I'm at work,' she said brightly. 'It feels like being on holiday!'

'I know what you mean,' said Rafe. 'We used to drive this way when I was taken to stay with my grandparents at Knighton Park as a kid, so the route reminds me of holidays too.'

Miranda could imagine Rafe as a little boy, dark-eyed and mischievous. 'Was it a family outing?'

'Not really. I'm an only child, and my parents were glad not to have me underfoot in the school holidays. Sometimes my mother would drive me down, but more often the chauffeur would take me, sitting in solitary splendour in the back of the car.'

Rafe's voice was light, but Miranda felt her heart twist. She would never have thought she would feel sorry for Rafe Knighton! Poor little boy.

'It sounds a bit lonely.'

'Oh, I didn't mind as long as I got there. I liked staying with my grandparents. It was more fun at Knighton Park than London. There were lots of places to get lost or get into trouble, or both, and I always seemed to find some other kids to play with.'

He probably started charming at a very early age, Miranda thought. It would have been one way of making sure that he always had a companion.

'What were your holidays like?' he asked her. 'I suppose you always had your sister to play with?' She seemed so self-sufficient that she could have been an only child too, but he remembered meeting Octavia, with her beauty and her ready smiles. He had been surprised that two such different girls could be related.

Now… He glanced at Miranda and remembered how she had looked when she smiled. If Octavia had closed her eyes and smiled languorously, would he have been as struck? Rafe thought not.

'Two sisters actually,' Miranda was saying. 'I'm the middle one.'

'Ah, three sisters…like a fairy tale?'

'Yes, but in the case of the Fairchilds, it's two beautiful sisters and one ugly one. Belinda looks like Octavia,' she added, just in case he hadn't realised who the ugly one was.

'You're not ugly,' said Rafe without thinking. 'You just dress badly. Every time I've seen you, you've been wearing a dull little suit like that one.'

That wasn't *quite* true, Miranda thought, and the memory of the cat suit sent faint colour creeping into her cheeks. Thank goodness he hadn't recognised her! It would have been mortifying.

'A suit's practical if you're working in an office,' she pointed out.

'There's nothing wrong with a suit if it's well cut, or if the colour is flattering, but you seem to go out of your way to pick bad designs and colours that do nothing at all for you,' he said almost crossly.

'You sound like my sisters!'

It was none of his business, Rafe knew, and probably deeply inappropriate to boot, but he had always had an eye for good design, and it bothered him that Miranda seemed to care so little about her appearance. It just seemed a *waste*.

'You dress as if you don't want anyone to notice you,' he grumbled.

Miranda sighed a little. 'That's probably true. Everyone else in my family was so flamboyant, and so obsessed with what they looked like, that I suppose I got used to not competing. I knew I could never look like my sisters, so it seemed easier not to even try.'

It couldn't be easy having one sister as spectacularly pretty as Octavia, let alone two, Rafe reflected. Still, it was a shame she didn't make more of herself. With a little effort, she could be lovely. You had to look twice to notice the luminous skin, to realise that the cool, quiet features were full of character, to see the intelligence shining in those steady eyes that seemed to waver between brown and green.

And that wasn't all. Rafe thought about the curl of her mouth as she smiled, about the way the ruthlessly confined hair gleamed with warmth in the sun.

'Why don't you let your hair down?' he demanded abruptly.

'You mean, why don't I have some fun?' said Miranda with an edge of bitterness. 'My sisters say that, too.'

'Actually, I meant literally,' said Rafe, 'but why not?'

'Literally, because it's more practical to have it tied back. Look what a mess it would be in now if it was hanging all over my face,' she pointed out. 'An open-topped sports car isn't the place to start experimenting with a new style, is it?'

'And not literally?'

She sighed. 'The only thing my family knew how to do was have fun,' she said. 'Look where fun has got me!'

There was a story there, thought Rafe, with a sidelong glance at her unguarded expression, but perhaps now was not the time to probe.

'Driving out of town on a sunny Monday morning?' he suggested.

Miranda acknowledged the point with a tiny huff of laughter. 'My Monday mornings aren't usually like this!'

'Mine either,' he agreed, 'so we might as well make the most of it. Let's get out of London, and then find somewhere to have that coffee. If Ginny found out I'd made you do without, I'd never hear the end of it!'

They were going against the traffic, so once they hit the motorway they made rapid progress. Rafe was a good driver, fast but not reckless, and his reactions were very quick. Conversation was difficult with the top down, but the further London fell behind them, the more Miranda's spirits rose.

It was a beautiful day, and she watched the countryside with pleasure as they sped by, but she was acutely conscious of Rafe beside her, long hands very steady on the steering wheel, dark hair ruffled by the wind, his thigh close enough to touch.

If things were different, she would be able to reach over and lay her hand on it, to feel how lean and warm and strong he was. If she were another girl, she would know how to touch him. If he were another man, he would smile and cover her hand possessively with his own.

If he were a man who loved her.

If he were a man she could love.

But he wasn't. He was Rafe Knighton, and he was the last man on earth she wanted to touch.

So why was her hand prickling and tingling with the mere thought of resting on his thigh? Uneasily, Miranda folded it against the other on her lap to keep it in place, and stared out at the landscape, but, instead of fields, Rafe's image danced maddeningly in front of her eyes, with that gleaming, heart-shaking smile and all the easy assurance of wealth and good looks.

Don't be an idiot, Miranda told herself firmly. Really, what was Rafe Knighton other than a walking, talking cliché? Tall, dark, handsome, impossibly rich…and vain and superficial and irresponsible and everything she despised.

No man like that was going to throw her into a tizzy, no matter how nice his smile.

Still, it was a relief when they stopped for coffee and she could get out of the car and put a bit more space between them.

They found a pub not far from the motorway, and sat at a table outside. A fat Labrador waddled out to keep them company in the sunshine. Miranda's face softened as he thrust his nose into her lap and wagged his tail.

'Hello, boy,' she said, fondling his ears, and Rafe was shocked to find himself thinking, for one ridiculous moment, Lucky dog.

'I love dogs,' she told him, looking up with a smile that made him wonder how he could ever have thought her colourless. 'I used to beg my parents for one, but they always said it would be too much trouble.'

'You'll get on well with my grandmother, then. She's got hordes of them! I prefer cats myself,' said Rafe, watching the way the dog was shedding hairs all over Miranda's skirt.

'Now, why does that not surprise me?' Miranda's voice was very dry. Cats spent their days pleasing themselves or grooming themselves. Easy to see why Rafe would identify with them!

'You've got to admit cats have style,' he said provocatively. It was interesting that she preferred dogs, he thought. She was so neat and self-contained so much of the time that he wouldn't have expected the noisy chaos that so often accompanied dogs to appeal to her. But she didn't seem at all bothered by the mess on her skirt.

'But dogs are so loyal and so reliable and so friendly,' Miranda was unable to resist arguing. 'Aren't you?' she added to the dog, who was panting happily back at her, wagging not just its tail but its entire back end.

As if to prove her point, it pulled its head out of her lap and went round to say hello to Rafe instead.

'Yes, yes, good dog,' he said, resigned, and gave it a pat.

It responded by resting its head adoringly on Rafe's knee and redoubling the wags.

'Come away now, Archie,' said the landlord sharply as he came out with their coffee on a tray. He put it down on the table, and pushed the dog away. 'Sorry, he loves people. Has he been bothering you?'

'Of course not. He's lovely,' Miranda assured him, but the landlord shooed the dog away anyway and left them to their coffee.

Turning back to Rafe, she saw him looking down at his trousers, where Archie had adoringly left a trail of slobber.

'Oh, for heaven's sake,' she said before he had a chance to launch into a diatribe against the messiness of dogs. 'It's just a bit of slobber! There's no need to make a fuss. Here.' She found a tissue in her bag and without thinking leant over to wipe his leg.

The breath hissed out of Rafe.

Miranda froze at the sound, then drew back, scarlet with

mortification. What was she *doing*? This was her boss. Knowing that it would be deeply inappropriate to touch him in any way, she had spent what felt like hours resisting the unprecedented temptation to lay her hand on his thigh in the car, and what did she do? Practically grab him and rub him down as if he were a child!

'I'm sorry,' she muttered. 'I wasn't thinking.'

Rafe didn't even hear her. 'It was you!' he said, staring.

'What?' Miranda looked at him uneasily.

Something about the way she tutted, something about the briskness with which she had leant over to wipe his trousers had switched on a light bulb of recognition in Rafe's brain. He remembered the waitress in the absurd cat suit brushing him down, the same way Miranda had brushed the traces of the dog from his trousers.

Exactly the same way.

Now he knew why the waitress had seemed vaguely familiar.

'You're that waitress who threw canapés all over me,' he said.

'It was an accident—' Miranda began in instinctive defence, and then stopped, furious with herself. Too late now to bluff it out and pretend that she didn't know what he was talking about!

'How did you recognise me?' she asked dully, looking away.

'Nobody mops up stains the way you do,' said Rafe, amusement quivering in his voice. Now that it was clear, he marvelled that he hadn't made the connection earlier. No one else walked with that straight-backed grace, did they? He should have recognised the proud tilt of her chin at least, the exasperated click of her tongue, the ironic curve of her mouth.

'I can't believe I didn't recognise you sooner,' he said. 'But you had your hair down, and you were wearing that mask…'

He trailed off, remembering what else she had been wearing that night, and he was dismayed to realise how vividly he could picture her in that tight-fitting cat suit. Who would have guessed that such a spectacular figure was hidden beneath the ill-fitting suits she wore?

In spite of himself, his eyes dropped to her legs. Encased in the cat suit, they had been long and slender. The dull grey skirt she wore now cut her off at the knee, but there was no mistaking those calves, those ankles. It was hard to believe that he had missed them until now.

Rafe swallowed.

It had been hard enough reconciling prim Miranda Fairchild, the efficient temp, with the woman who had smiled so sensuously in the sunshine, without knowing that she was also a cat-suit-wearing waitress with a figure that had lingered in his memory far longer than it should.

How was he to deal with her now?

'You let your hair down when you're waitressing,' he found himself saying absurdly.

'Only when the client insists.' Miranda looked defensive. She sat very straight, feeling exposed. She might as well still have been wearing that cat suit. 'We don't normally have to wear those stupid costumes.'

'Do you get hassled like that a lot?' he asked uncomfortably, remembering the casual way that man had touched her and wished he'd thumped him when he had the chance.

She smiled a little wryly. 'Nobody has ever noticed me at all,' she said. 'Those cat suits were deliberately provocative— I wasn't the only waitress who had problems that night—but that's the first and last time we've ever had to wear anything like that. Normally I just wear a regular uniform.'

Rafe wished she'd been wearing a regular uniform the other evening. Knowing what a gorgeous figure she had under those shapeless suits of hers wasn't going to help his concentration at all!

His throat was dry. Miranda's knees were tugging at the edge of his vision, but he mustn't stare. Nobody's ever noticed me, wasn't that what she had said? If only *he* hadn't noticed her. Now that he had, Rafe was very much afraid that he wasn't going to be able to stop.

Which was absurd. It wasn't as if she had turned into a raving beauty. She was still cool and prim, and her hair was still tied back in that ugly style. All he had to do was forget about how she had looked in that cat suit.

All?

Hah.

'I didn't realise you had an evening job,' he said, conscious that he sounded lame, but he who was never at a loss for a flip comment was suddenly as tongue-tied as a boy and unable to think of anything to say.

Miranda leaned forward to pour the coffee. 'It's not a problem, is it?'

'No, no,' he said hastily. 'It must be tiring, though, working all day and then starting another job in the evening.'

'It is, but I need the money. Temping doesn't pay well, even when you're working somewhere like the Knighton Group.'

'Couldn't you get a permanent job?' Rafe took the cup she passed to him with a murmur of thanks. 'It's obvious that you're more than capable. Simon told me you'd have been able to run Communications by yourself by the time you'd been there a week. You ought to be a manager or administrator at the very least.'

'Unfortunately, I don't have much of a CV.' Miranda stirred her coffee mindlessly. She had been over and over this so many times.

'You learnt to organise somewhere,' Rafe pointed out. 'How old are you? Twenty-nine? Thirty?'

A faint flush stained her cheekbones. 'Twenty-seven.'

'Then you've been doing *something* for the past ten years. Even if you don't have qualifications, you must have experience.'

'Only of failure,' she said bleakly, her eyes on her coffee.

'You surprise me,' he said. 'You strike me as so competent I would have said that you would make a success of whatever you did.'

Miranda's mouth twisted. If only he knew! 'I'm afraid it would have taken a lot more than competence to rescue Fairchild's.'

Rafe raised his brows. He remembered Fairchild's from his childhood. A long-established chain of department stores, the shops had disappeared from London years ago. He had heard the company had gone belly up the year before but he'd been in Africa at the time and didn't know any details.

'You're one of *those* Fairchilds?'

She nodded. 'Looking back, I can see that the firm had been going steadily downhill for years, but I didn't realise how badly until I went to university. I'd only been there a year when it became obvious it was in big trouble. My father was struggling, and there was no one else to help him.' Miranda lifted her shoulders helplessly at the memory. 'I dropped out and went to work with him instead. I thought I could make a difference but...'

'What happened?'

'We didn't innovate. We didn't develop. We didn't recognise that the world had changed and we had to change with it.' She sighed, remembering.

'It sounds as if *you* did.'

'I wasn't enough,' she said with a trace of bitterness. 'I couldn't persuade my father that we had to do things differently. Perhaps it was too late, anyway. It would have taken a complete transformation to turn things round, and my father wasn't the only one convinced that our reputation would see us through.'

'Reputation is a two-edged sword,' said Rafe thoughtfully. 'It can work to your advantage, sure, but it can be a huge liability, too. Once it's established, it's almost impossible to change the way people think of you.'

He glanced down at Miranda, and his smile gleamed suddenly, burning behind her eyelids. 'I should know,' he said.

She looked away. She had an uncomfortable feeling that *she* was changing the way she thought about him.

'So what happened in the end?' he asked after a moment. 'Were you taken over?'

'No, there were some offers, but my father refused to consider any of them.' He had never accepted the reality of the situation, Miranda remembered, but had insisted on hanging onto the trappings of wealth long after the substance of it had been squandered.

'Then he had a heart attack, and died, and by then it was too late. The firm just collapsed in on itself. We were declared bankrupt, and that was it. I did what I could for the employees, but it wasn't much, and then I had to find a job for myself, which wasn't that easy. I'm not exactly employable.'

Her face was set, her mouth pressed firmly together, and glancing down at her Rafe was struck by the mixture of strength and vulnerability in her expression. It couldn't have been an easy time for her, and obviously the sense of failure ran deep, but she had evidently picked herself up and started again, right back at the bottom. That took guts.

'So you became a temp?'

'I had to do something,' she pointed out. 'We had to sell everything. My father wasn't very savvy about money—probably because it had always just been there for him—so he'd never considered setting up trusts or transferring ownership of the houses, or even taking out life insurance.'

Rafe grimaced. It sounded as if her father had been completely feckless. 'Leaving you with nothing?'

'Leaving me with what most of us have, the ability to earn my own living,' said Miranda sharply. She hated people feeling sorry for her. 'I'm really lucky to have a good friend who's let me rent a room in her flat at a ridiculously cheap rate, and since I signed on with an agency, I've got an income. Things could be a lot worse.'

It must have been hard for her nonetheless, Rafe thought, pitched from a life of wealth and privilege into the day-to-day grind of working for a living and scraping by from one pay day to the next. One moment she had been a board member, the next she was a lowly temp, reduced to wrestling with photocopiers.

Miranda puffed out a sigh and leant forward to put the cup and saucer back on the tray. 'I just feel so sad about Fairchild's,' she confessed. 'My great-grandfather started the firm, and my grandfather built it up to a household name. They both worked so hard to make it a great firm. We just let all that go to waste.'

It was a pity she hadn't had longer, Rafe thought. She might have been able to turn things round, but it sounded as if her father had frittered away his inheritance long before she tried to take the reins.

'Companies have natural life cycles,' he said comfortingly. 'Three generations isn't a bad run. It's a classic pattern: one generation to make a fortune, one to consolidate it, and one to spend it. It happens a lot.'

'It hasn't happened to Knighton's.'

'No,' Rafe admitted. 'I'm the fourth generation, and I don't intend to be the one to let it fall apart either, in spite of what everyone thinks.'

His expression had hardened, and when Miranda looked at him she saw that his mouth was set. Deep inside her, something shivered into life for a brief moment before she suppressed it firmly.

'Then should you be out wasting time on a Monday thinking about a ball?'

'The ball is part of my strategy.'

Rafe put down his own coffee and leant back, stretching his

arms along the back of the bench. He wasn't touching Miranda at all, but she was desperately aware of his hand behind her shoulder. He seemed to be taking up an awful lot of space, and she found herself stiffening and edging along the bench.

'Strategy?' Her voice was humiliatingly thin and high, and she cleared her throat. 'What strategy?' she tried again.

'What do you know about me?'

Miranda hesitated. 'What do you mean?'

'Had you ever heard about me before I caught you abusing that photocopier?'

She would have loved to have denied it, but she had never been any good at lying. 'Of course.'

'So what am I like? Go on, there's no need to be polite,' said Rafe. 'What do the gossip columns say about me?'

'Well…that you're a playboy, I suppose. You're wild and extravagant and very rich. You go out with lots of beautiful women.'

'That's it?'

'I don't know what you want me to say. You seem to have an incredible jet set life, skiing with movie stars and sailing in the Caribbean with models. You know, just the same old, same old.'

'But what do I *do*?'

'Nothing.'

There was a tiny pause. 'Right, so I just drift around going to parties and sleeping with a lot of women, is that it?'

Miranda bristled a little at his tone. 'I haven't seen you do anything else,' she pointed out. 'The first time I met you, you were wandering around the office as if you didn't know what to do with yourself. Then you were at that stupid party with a model hanging on your arm. This morning I came in to work for you, and the first thing you do is drive off in a sports car to have lunch in the country and talk about a ball.'

'Hmm, it doesn't sound good when you put it like that.'

'How would *you* put it?'

'I wander round the office so I get to know how the different departments work and who does what. I only went to that party because it was a book launch, and I thought I might meet some interesting people there—wrong, I know! I'd never met Kyra before that evening, and I didn't sleep with her, and today...well, this is part of my plan to change my reputation.'

'I think you might have to work a bit harder to do that!'

CHAPTER FOUR

'THE board think like you do,' said Rafe, and to Miranda's relief he dropped his arms and leant forward to rest them on his knees instead. 'They think like my father did. They're horrified at the idea of me taking over Knighton's, but there isn't much they can do about it yet. They're hoping that if they give me enough time, I'll screw up, and then they'll be able to get rid of me, but I don't intend to do that.'

'What are you going to do about it?'

'It's clear that I'm never going to get anywhere as long as they think I'm just the spoilt party boy I used to be,' said Rafe. 'I know I was wild. I made plenty of mistakes, and I'm sorry for them, but I'm not that boy any more. I've accepted responsibility for the stupid things I've done, and moved on. Now all I want is for the board, and everyone else, to recognise that.'

'It's hard to change people's expectations of you,' said Miranda, thinking of her own family. For as long as she could remember, she had been the sensible, practical sister, the one the others relied on to sort things out and deal with any problems, and she couldn't imagine Belinda or Octavia ever thinking of her as any different. She couldn't imagine *being* any different now.

'We get pigeon-holed as a certain type of person quite early on, and sometimes it's difficult to know whether we're really that person, or whether we become that person just because that's how everyone expects us to be.'

'*Exactly.*' Rafe's eyes lit with relief as he turned to look at her. She was the first person who had ever understood.

'My father always thought of me as an irresponsible boy, so that's the way I was for a long time,' he told her. 'I got a degree, but everyone just assumed that it was given to me on a plate, and I knew that if I got a job, they would all think the same. My father didn't trust me with any responsibility at Knighton's, so I ended up messing around, taking stupid risks and behaving badly and generally being determined to live down to my father's expectations.'

Miranda shifted a little uncomfortably. She had never troubled to think about why Rafe might have behaved as he had. She had been like everyone else, damning him on appearances, and assuming that anyone showered with wealth and privilege and good looks must have the easiest of existences.

Rafe was shaking his head ruefully at the memory of his younger self. 'The trouble is that a single-minded pursuit of fun and excitement wears pretty thin after a while. It isn't a very satisfying way to live. One day I realised that I'd had enough of it. I knew I would never change what my father thought of me, but I could change what I thought about myself.'

She studied him thoughtfully. Changing how you thought about yourself probably wasn't nearly as easy as it sounded. 'How did you do that?'

'I went to work as a volunteer setting up micro-finance projects in West Africa. I'm not completely useless,' he said, reading Miranda's astonished expression without difficulty. 'I studied economics at university and I did actually read some books.'

'Yes, but...' Miranda had been expecting him to say that he had gone travelling perhaps, or done some trendy self-development course. She lifted her hands in a helpless gesture, unable to express what she thought. 'I'd no idea,' she said at last.

'No one has. They all think I've been partying for the past four years.'

Having assumed precisely the same thing, Miranda had the grace to blush. 'I can't imagine you in Africa.'

'Why not?'

'Because of the way you dress, I suppose.' She gestured at him. Even in jeans and a casual shirt, he looked immaculate. 'You're always so…well groomed.'

He looked amused. 'You wouldn't have thought that if you'd seen me there, I promise you.'

Perhaps not, but Miranda was prepared to bet he had never looked hot and sticky and crumpled and dusty the way she surely would if she had to work in the crushing heat.

'What was it like out there?'

'Africa? I loved it.' Rafe's voice was warm with enthusiasm. 'I met so many wonderful people and learnt so much. It was the best thing I've ever done.'

Miranda tried to picture him in a dusty African village, but it was hard. He was too much *there*, beside her, looking as if he had stepped out of an ad for designer clothes. He was leaning back once more, long legs stretched out in front of him and crossed at the ankle. His shirt was rolled up to reveal powerful-looking forearms covered in fine dark hairs, and the open neck revealed a strong brown throat.

Her eyes flickered to his profile, to the forceful lines of his cheek and jaw and the cool curl of his mouth, and a disturbing warmth quivered into life deep inside her. He was so strong, so solid. How could she ever have dismissed him as little more than a clothes horse? This was no wild boy with nothing to recommend him but his looks and his charm. This was a powerful man whose magnetism ran far deeper than the clothes he wore.

Suddenly breathless, Miranda made herself look away. 'Why did you come back if you loved it so much?' Amazingly, her voice came out perfectly normal.

'My father died.' Rafe's expression sobered. 'We've got that in common. Both our fathers have died recently. Whatever his private doubts about me, mine left me a controlling share in the Knighton Group. I wish I'd come back before he died so he could see what I'd learnt and how I'd changed, but we always think there'll be time enough...'

His voice trailed off and he lifted a shoulder as if trying to shrug off regret. 'I thought he was so disappointed in me that he might have made other arrangements, but he was a believer in duty and family and perhaps he wanted to give me a chance.'

'Or perhaps he just loved you and wanted to leave you everything he had?'

Rafe's smile was crooked. 'Perhaps. Either way, he's entrusted me with the group, and it feels as if keeping the company successful is my responsibility now. It's something I need to do for him, and want to do for myself. I hadn't realised how much the firm means to me until I came back. It's in my blood, I suppose.'

'It must have been a bit of a shock taking over a company like Knightons, after working in villages,' said Miranda, still trying to come to terms with this new, disturbing knowledge of him. She felt completely thrown.

She wished she didn't know what he had been doing for the past four years. She wished she could still think of him as spoilt and superficial. She wished she hadn't noticed the pulse beating in his throat and the texture of his skin and the power of his long, lean body. It had been easier before.

Swallowing, she reminded herself sternly that she was here in a professional capacity, no matter how unlikely a sunny pub garden might be as a workplace. This was her job, and for now

Rafe was her boss. It would be inappropriate to feel attracted to him, physically or otherwise.

Inappropriate, and completely pointless.

It was depressing to realise that she was at risk of becoming a walking, talking cliché herself. Surely she knew better than to fall for her boss, no matter how attractive he might be? And surely—*surely*—she knew there was no point in even hoping that he might ever find her attractive in return?

Get real, Miranda told herself. You're not Octavia. You're plain and prissy and practical, and there's no way a man like Rafe Knighton is ever going to look at you as more than an efficient secretary. Don't be so silly.

'It was. It still is,' said Rafe ruefully recalling his initial culture shock on his first day back at Knighton's.

To Miranda's relief, he seemed completely unaware of her jittering with awareness beside him. Perhaps he was used to women going weak at the knees when he was near? The thought that she risked being one of such a large crowd stiffened Miranda's spine. She was *not* going to be like all the others. If an efficient assistant was all he wanted, that was what she would be.

'But I'm not going to give in,' he was continuing. 'I know the board are sitting there like vultures, waiting for me to make a mistake before swooping in, but I'm not going to let them.' His jaw set in a resolute line. 'They think I'm still the boy my father thought I was right to the end. I just have to prove them wrong.'

'How are you going to do that?' Miranda was proud of her cool tone. She had herself back under control after that rather embarrassing little wobble, which she blamed entirely on her hormones. It must be the time of the month. She wasn't normally that silly.

'I'm going to get married.'

'*Married!*' In complete defiance of the fact that it was supposed to be firmly under control, Miranda's heart lurched into her throat, performed a sickening somersault and landed splat back between her ribs. 'Congratulations,' she managed after a moment. 'I didn't realise you were engaged.'

'I'm not,' said Rafe. 'Yet. But I'd like to be.' He grinned at her. 'That's where you come in.'

Off went her heart again, blundering around her chest. Don't be ridiculous, Miranda told herself. Rafe wasn't suggesting marrying *her*.

'I'm not sure I understand,' she said carefully.

Rafe sat up straighter. 'I came home to take over the Knighton Group, and I'm glad I did,' he said. 'The company and its success are important to me. It's not my capability that's the problem, it's trying to get people to take me seriously and acknowledge that I've changed. I feel as if I'm beating my head against the proverbial brick wall, hoping that my directors will recognise who I am now, not who I was even four years ago.'

'It might take some time to change their views.' Miranda looked doubtful.

'I know, but I don't want to wait thirty years before they get the message. I need to do something more dramatic now. That's where getting married comes in.'

'I don't see how,' she admitted. 'It's not as if you'd be marrying your directors.'

'It's about perception,' said Rafe. 'If I appear to be more settled, I think that would make a difference. And I'm thirty-five. I'm ready to settle down and be taken seriously. My grandmother was nagging me to do it four years ago, but I was too restless then. I feel differently now. I want to get married, start a family, concentrate on making Knighton's an even better company than it is already.'

'Then what's the problem?'

'I can't find anyone to marry.'

Miranda laughed.

'No, really,' he said.

'Oh, come on! You're Britain's most eligible bachelor! They must be queuing up to marry you.' Octavia certainly was, she reflected.

'That's just the trouble,' said Rafe. 'Of course I meet plenty of women, but they're not the kind of women I want to marry.'

When Miranda raised her brows, he went on. 'Since I came home, I've been invited to all the same parties, where I meet all the same people I used to know, but I can't be bothered with them any more. I can't believe that was all my life was, just an endless round of social events.

'It's not enough any more,' he told her. 'I'm looking for something more... more *interesting*, some*one* more interesting.'

'Well, that shouldn't be too difficult,' said Miranda. It was hard to believe that someone like Rafe would be lonely for long.

'I didn't think it would be either,' said Rafe frankly, 'but it's certainly not as easy as I expected. The trouble is, I only get invited to the kind of occasions where the paparazzi are hanging around outside the door, and it's all about celebrity and being seen. I don't want to marry a model or a TV personality or a party girl with a trust fund to support her. If I'm going to spend my life with someone, I want her to be someone with a little more substance, with her own ambitions, her own opinions, her own interests. I want her to be a serious person, and serious people don't go to the kind of parties I go to at the moment.'

Oh, dear. It wasn't looking good for Octavia.

But who was she to talk? A temp who moonlighted as a cocktail waitress in a cat suit hardly ranked as a serious person either. Miranda was very glad she had decided not to do anything silly like falling for Rafe herself. Whatever wife Rafe had in mind, it wasn't going to be anyone like her.

'So I've decided to do something about it,' Rafe announced. 'I know the right woman for me is out there somewhere. I've just got to stop hoping I'll stumble across her and go out and find her instead. And *then* I've got to persuade her not to hold my reputation against me.'

Privately, Miranda couldn't see that being much of a problem. Few women, no matter how high-minded, were going to be immune to a handsome, single, straight, wealthy man, let alone one who was looking for long-term commitment.

But it wasn't her job to pander to Rafe Knighton's ego.

'So you're just going to find someone serious and then marry her?'

'Of course not,' he said. 'All I want is the chance to meet more people and hope that I might find someone I find attractive and interesting among them. I want to try and change people's perception of me. And that's where the ball comes in. I want to invite serious women.'

'What, so you can inspect them as if you're at a smorgasbord and take your pick?' said Miranda, unimpressed.

'How else am I to meet them?' he countered reasonably. 'And I won't just invite women, of course. I'm not that crass. I just want to meet a more interesting mix of people. Is that too much to ask?'

'You don't think it will reinforce your reputation as a party guy?' she asked. 'A ball is a pretty frivolous idea, after all.'

'I'm thinking of it as a bridge between my two different worlds,' said Rafe. 'I still like people, and I like socialising, but that's not all there is to me. Sure, I'll invite some glamorous friends, but it's not going to be all empty-headed celebrities. I want people to know that there is a more serious side to me too.

'Yes, it's a party,' he went on, surprised at how anxious he was to convince Miranda that the ball was a good idea, 'but it will also be a fund-raising event in aid of the projects I worked on in Africa. A serious cause should appeal to serious people, serious *women*, real women doing real jobs, but not so serious that they can't enjoy themselves. So I'll invite women who work in development and funding agencies, with solicitors and doctors and engineers, publishers and academics and journalists—the responsible ones, anyway. You get the idea...'

Among all those interesting, capable women, there were bound to be some who were also attractive and sweet and ready to be fallen in love with, surely?

'If nothing else, it will raise a lot of money for a very good cause.'

Rafe paused, wondering if Miranda understood how important this was to him. 'That's why it has to be properly organised. I want you to set it up, and target invitations to make sure a good cross-section of people come. I'll need you to liaise with the projects in Africa too, and make sure the money goes where it's needed.'

'It's a bigger job than I thought,' said Miranda slowly, still not entirely convinced about the idea but unable to think of any real objections.

'It'll be good experience if you want to improve that CV,' he pointed out with an unfair smile.

'True,' said Miranda, resisting it like mad.

Rafe got to his feet. 'Well, the first thing is to find somewhere to have the ball, so let's go and see the ballroom at Knighton Park, and take it from there.'

Knighton Park wasn't quite the monstrosity that Rafe had described, but it was certainly enormous. It was a vast, rambling Victorian house built in the Gothic style, complete with turrets, battlements, and an imposing gatehouse. Its walls were half smothered in ivy, and what the house lacked in beauty it made up for in size, with two massive wings flanking the central façade.

'Gosh,' said Miranda as the car crunched to a halt on the thick gravel. She was used to grand houses, but this one was something special.

Rafe laughed. 'It's an acquired taste, I know, but I'm fond of it.'

'Will you live here once you're married?'

He rested his hands on the steering wheel and looked at the house. 'I hadn't thought about it, to be honest,' he said slowly. 'I suppose it depends on my grandmother and how she gets on with my bride. She can be a bit…intimidating, but her bark is usually worse than her bite.'

A posse of little dogs jumped up, yapping, as a smiling house-keeper showed them into a sunny sitting room overlooking the gardens at the back of the house. Muttering under his breath, Rafe stepped through them to greet his grandmother, who was rising from her chair, while Miranda stooped to say hello to the dogs.

When she extricated herself from their greetings, Elvira Knighton had turned from her grandson and was watching her with keen eyes. She was stooped with rheumy eyes and gnarled hands that glittered with diamonds, but Miranda could see from her bone structure that she had once been a great beauty.

'Miranda is here on a special assignment,' Rafe explained when he had introduced them. 'I've decided that you're right, and that it's time I got married.'

Elvira's brows shot up as she turned to look at Miranda once more.

'Not me,' Miranda said hastily, holding up both hands. 'I'm just the hired help!'

'I'm planning a ball, Elvira,' said Rafe, and explained his plan to his grandmother, who listened carefully. When he had finished, she looked at Miranda.

'Hmmph,' was all she said.

'Have we got time to look at the ballroom before lunch?' asked Rafe.

'Yes, yes, off you go.' She waved him away as if irritated. 'Don't be late back, though.'

'She likes you,' Rafe said to Miranda as he led her to the ballroom.

'How on earth can you tell that?'

'She was watching you while you were talking to all those yappy little dogs.'

'They're not yappy. They were just being friendly.'

'That's what she says.'

Rafe stopped and threw open some double doors. 'This is the ballroom. What do you think?'

Slowly, Miranda stepped inside.

Stretching almost the entire length of one wing, the ballroom was lined all along one side with full-length windows opening onto a terrace, and from there steps led in their turn onto a sweep of lawn. The walls were painted cream, the floor was polished. Dust motes danced in the sunlight striping through the long windows and dulled the sparkle of the chandeliers.

The whole room echoed with the ghosts of balls past, and Miranda narrowed her eyes, almost able to see the couples twirling around the floor, hear the beat of the music and the swish of silk dresses, smell the perfume adrift on the air, and feel the frisson of bodies moving together, palms touching.

'It's perfect,' she said.

Rafe let out a long breath. He hadn't realised how much he had been hoping that she would like it.

'We'll need a band,' he said.

Miranda nodded, still caught up in the atmosphere. 'It would be lovely to have a traditional ball, with an orchestra. It's a pity nobody knows how to waltz any more,' she said.

'I know how to waltz,' Rafe objected.

'You *do*?'

'Of course. Don't you?'

She shook her head. 'No. I've never learnt how to dance.'

'I'll show you,' said Rafe, taking her hand before she had time to protest, and swinging her into the middle of the floor.

'Oh, no—' Miranda broke off breathless as he pulled her back towards him, smiling, and caught her by the waist to draw her against him. 'I didn't mean…'

He ignored her attempts to protest. 'You'll probably find this difficult,' he said conversationally. 'It means following me. For once you're not going to be the one that takes responsibility and decides what to do.'

'Now, look,' she began, but the rest of her protest died on her lips. She was too flustered by his warm hand around hers, by the nearness of his body, the feel of his hand pressing against the small of her back, holding her close.

'Relax,' Rafe instructed. 'You're too tense.'

Of course she was tense! How could she not be tense when her heart was thudding and her nerves were fizzing and her whole body was thrumming with his nearness?

Rafe could feel her slender and rigid in his arms. She refused to meet his eyes. It wasn't fair to tease her, but she smelt fresh and clean, and when he looked down he could see the arch of her brows drawn together in a disapproving line and the sweep of her lowered lashes. Her bottom lip was caught between her teeth, and something tightened inside him at the sight.

Humming off key, he swept Miranda around the dusty floor. 'You don't need to think,' he assured her. 'Just follow my steps.'

It was so ridiculous that after a moment Miranda started to laugh. It was ridiculous and yet somehow magical and exhilarating too as he twirled her round and round the dusty floor. Once she stopped trying to work it out for herself and simply gave herself up to him, letting him move her, it was much easier.

She was breathless and still laughing by the time Rafe spun her in a final circle and let her go, retaining a firm grasp of her hand so that he could bow low.

'There,' he said, not sounding at all breathless. 'That wasn't so hard, was it?'

Their eyes met for a moment and Miranda felt her heart flip alarmingly.

'This isn't getting the ball organised,' she said, trying to sound severe but instead she could hear that her voice was high and tight.

'Just getting in the mood,' said Rafe, thrown by an unexpected clench of desire. She had felt surprisingly right in his arms, warm and slender, and when she laughed up at him something tightened around his heart.

'You were getting the hang of it,' he said. 'Imagine what you could do if there was music! You'll have to keep a dance for me at the ball.'

'I won't be dancing,' said Miranda, pulling her hand away at last and stepping back. 'I'll be working, remember? And you'll be on the lookout for a bride.'

Rafe had forgotten that for a moment. She was right.

'So I will,' he said.

There was a tiny pause.

'Well,' he said a little too heartily. 'Let's go and ask Elvira if we can borrow her ballroom.'

They had lunch sitting round one end of a vast dining table, with portraits of Rafe's ancestors staring ponderously down at them.

'I don't normally eat here,' Elvira explained, 'but it's important to keep up standards when I have guests.'

'I'm hardly a guest,' said Rafe humorously.

'Miranda is.' His grandmother inspected her with a disconcertingly sharp gaze as she unfolded her napkin. 'Fairchild? Any relation to the department store Fairchilds?'

'Yes, except there are no stores any longer, I'm afraid.'

'I remember your father, in that case. A charming boy, but not much grit.' Elvira's eyes narrowed in an effort of memory.

'Didn't he marry one of the Tatton girls? There were about four of them, all beauties, but one of them was a bolter, as I recall.'

Miranda's smile didn't falter. 'My mother,' she said, and Rafe winced for her. 'She ran off with a racehorse trainer when I was twelve.'

Anyone else would have been embarrassed by the faux pas, but not his grandmother. Not a whit discomposed, Elvira studied Miranda's face thoughtfully. 'You don't look much like either of your parents from what I can remember.'

'No, I'm afraid not. My sisters are both very beautiful, though.'

'Probably a good thing. You've got character instead.' Elvira turned to her grandson. 'Why don't you marry Miranda?'

'Elvira!' Rafe threw Miranda an apologetic look. 'Miranda's here as my assistant, not a girlfriend!'

'You said you wanted to get married, didn't you?'

'Well, yes, but—'

'What's the point of going to all the expense and effort of a ball if you've got a perfectly nice girl right in front of you?'

Miranda was quite enjoying seeing Rafe put on the spot by his forceful grandmother, but she could see a muscle working in Rafe's jaw and decided it was time she intervened.

'It's nice of you to think of me,' she said politely, 'but I don't want to marry Rafe.'

'Why not?' Elvira looked positively affronted. 'He's clean, and healthy, and not such an idiot as he looks! Plenty of money, too. He'd be a good catch for you.'

In spite of himself, Rafe grinned. 'Elvira, stop, you're making me blush!' he said. 'You'll turn my head with all these compliments.'

Miranda bit back a smile. 'I'm sure he'll make someone an excellent husband, but it won't be me. I've got other plans.'

'Is there someone else?'

'No,' she admitted. 'But I don't want to live in London. I'm saving up to restore an old cottage by the sea. I'm going to live there and set up my own business and be as self-sufficient as I can. I can't imagine it would be the sort of life that would suit Rafe at all.'

'I'm sorry about my grandmother,' said Rafe as they left after lunch. 'She can be a bit direct!'

'I didn't mind,' said Miranda, clicking her seat belt into place. 'I liked her.'

There was silence for a moment. Rafe put the car into gear and set off down the long avenue of mature trees. He was frowning slightly.

'Was it true what you said?'

She looked at him in surprise. 'What about?'

'About there not being anyone else?'

'Oh, that.' She settled back into her seat. 'Of course. How long do you think "anyone else" lasts once they've set eyes on my sister? I used to get asked out a lot, but any prospective boyfriends usually just wanted to meet Octavia, or Belinda until she was married. I gave up accepting invitations in the end.'

'You mean you've never had a serious boyfriend?'

'Well, there was Keith. I met him when I went to university. Predictably, I reacted against my upbringing and chose someone I knew my father would disapprove of. Keith was a socialist and took his politics very seriously.'

Miranda's reminiscent smile was crooked. 'I was absolutely sure he'd be immune to Belinda, who was the ultimate It girl then. Octavia was still at school then, fortunately, but Keith took one look at Belinda, and that was it. I vowed to never take anyone home after that, but I had to give up my course and join the firm anyway the next year, so that was that.'

Rafe made a face. 'So you've given up on men?'

'No, I'm just facing reality. I'm not the kind of girl men

lose their heads over. It would be nice to think that one day I'd meet someone who didn't care what I looked like, but in the meantime I've got other things,' she said resolutely. 'I've got my dream.'

'Doing up that old cottage?' Rafe didn't sound impressed.

'It's all I want at the moment. Why do you think I'm temping, and spending my evenings passing round plates of canapés? I hate it in London,' said Miranda more passionately than he had heard her before. 'I can't breathe there, and it's got too many bad memories. I can't wait to leave it behind!'

At the end of the avenue, they passed the lodge and went through the imposing gates Rafe's great-grandfather had built to show the world that he had arrived. Rafe waited for a tractor to pass and then turned onto the narrow country road.

'If you hate London that much, why don't you just move out now?'

Miranda sighed. 'Because I'm too practical. I inherited the cottage from my godmother, but it's in poor condition. I don't mind living rough but I'll have to get the basics done, and that will cost a bit. I can earn more in London than I could elsewhere, and as long as I can live cheaply with Rosie I can save my earnings as a waitress. If nothing else, I'd need some money to live on until I can get a business up and running.'

'What kind of business?'

Miranda looked away. 'I don't know,' she admitted, shamefaced. 'It's all too far in the future to imagine very clearly. I don't want to think about how long it's going to be before I can afford to even think about moving out of London, so I'm just holding onto the idea of it at the moment. I hardly ever get down there as it is. Whitestones is surprisingly isolated, and you need a car to get there. I can't afford to hire one at the moment.'

'Then we'd better go now,' said Rafe as they came up to the main road. 'Which way?'

'It's miles from here!' Miranda protested, although the thought of seeing Whitestones again tugged yearningly at her.

'It can't be that far. We said we'd go to sea,' he pointed out. 'It's only half past two. It's too early to go back, but too late to do anything useful with the day if we do. Besides, I'd like to see this place of yours.'

'Well, if you're sure…' Succumbing to temptation, Miranda leant forward and pointed right. 'That way.'

The closer they got to the coast, the higher her spirits rose. She hadn't been to Whitestones since Rosie had driven her down for one bitterly cold day just after Christmas and she was excited to see the cottage again.

Rafe pretended concern as she directed him down twisting country lanes. 'Where exactly are we going, Miranda? I feel as if I'm about to drive off the edge of the earth!'

'I told you it was isolated.'

Isolated it certainly was. Miranda showed him where to pull over in a rough patch of grass next to a gate. If he parked right up against the hedge, another car could get by if necessary…although Rafe couldn't imagine why anyone else would be there.

He stretched and looked around him as he got out of the car. 'Where's the cottage?'

'Over there.' Miranda pointed across a field. 'We have to walk from here.'

She led the way through the gate and cut across the field. Rafe followed gingerly. The sun was shining today but it had been a wet spring and the field was still muddy. Before he was halfway across, the bottoms of his jeans were spattered with mud and his beautifully shined shoes were unrecognisable.

Miranda's court shoes were faring even worse. 'Oh, dear, I suppose we're not very suitably dressed,' she said, looking down at her prim office suit and then at Rafe, who pretended to look stern.

'It had better be worth it!' he said, but she could see the telltale tug at the corner of his mouth, and she smiled back, suddenly sure.

'It will be,' she promised.

CHAPTER FIVE

ACROSS a stream on a rickety bridge, up a path through some trees and finally they were there. Whitestones was a long, low, sturdy cottage with a glassed-in verandah overlooking the sea, and a cluster of outbuildings at the back. It had a wonderful situation, nestled into a slight hollow for shelter, but opening out to the glittering expanse of the English Channel.

Oh, yes, the setting was spectacular, but Rafe was aghast when Miranda showed him round the house. She had retrieved a key from its hiding place and opened the door with apparent pride. Inside, it was damp and dingy and dusty and dilapidated. Its paint was peeling, its plaster cracked. There was no phone, no heating, no water and no mains electricity.

'Dulcie, my godmother, managed with a generator, and used to pump water by hand,' Miranda explained.

'I hope you're not planning to do the same?'

'I will until I can afford to do something about it. Dulcie lived here on her own until she was sixty. If she could do it, I can.'

'But, Miranda…' Rafe began to protest, until he remembered that it wasn't any of his business.

'It needs some work, I know.' Miranda opened the verandah door so they could sit on the steps leading down to the garden. She could see that Rafe was appalled, and tried to look at the cottage through his eyes. It wasn't in a good state. A house needed to be lived in and cared for, but what could she do?

'I wish you could have seen it when Dulcie was here,' she told him. 'I suppose it was always a bit shabby, but it was warm and clean and it always seemed to be full of sunshine.'

Her expression softened with memory as she rested her elbows on her knees and propped her chin on her curled fists. 'I used to love coming to stay with her. I'm always surprised my parents chose her as my godmother. She wasn't anything like them. She was at school with my mother, I think, but they couldn't have been more different. I don't think my mother ever came here, in fact, but if she did she would have hated it.

'Belinda and Octavia did. They thought it was boring, and that Dulcie was eccentric, so I used to come on my own, and that was fine by me. I never felt as if I fitted in with my own family,' Miranda went on, 'but I felt right at home here with Dulcie. She never cared what I looked like. She never criticised me because I wasn't dressed properly or hadn't spent hours fiddling with my hair. She never expected me to pick up after her or make sure she got somewhere on time. She just expected me to be myself.'

Her voice cracked, just a little, and when Rafe glanced at her he saw that her lips were pressed together in a tight line.

'She sounds like a nice godmother to have.'

'She was wonderful. I always had interesting conversations with Dulcie,' Miranda remembered. 'She never talked down to me. Even when I was a very little girl I can remember her treating me as if I were an adult.

'Generally, though, Dulcie preferred animals to humans,' she went on. 'She was always rescuing them and nursing them back to health. I remember the cottage being full of cats and rabbits and chickens and hedgehogs and baby birds…and of course all sorts of dogs. Rafferty was my favourite.'

She smiled reminiscently. 'He was an Irish Setter cross who'd been abandoned on the road. I loved that dog,' said Miranda. 'I walked him for hours.'

Rafe studied her dreamy profile. She had told him more about herself than perhaps she realised. Growing up as an ugly duckling in a family of self-absorbed beauties—including her father, by the sound of it—it was hardly surprising that she had retreated behind that prickly, prim, practical façade.

It was odd now to remember how colourless she had seemed when he first met her. Rafe watched her now, sitting on the steps in her neat grey skirt and that good girl white blouse and her muddy shoes. She was different here. He had been able to tell as soon as she got out of the car. Even sitting there he could see that those taut muscles had relaxed. It was as if the sea and the air and this dilapidated old house had lit something inside her.

She was almost shining with it, he thought. Miranda would never be pretty, but she reminded him of a bright-eyed bird with deceptively dowdy plumage, the subtle beauty of whose patterned feathers you only saw when you looked closely.

No, not a beauty, and yet…Rafe remembered how light and slender she had been in his arms as he danced her around the dusty ballroom. The clean, fresh fragrance of her still lingered in his memory, like the gurgle of laughter and the smile that had lit up her face, and, more disturbingly, that peculiar sense of *rightness* he had felt when he held her.

Rafe shook the thought aside. Really, he was getting fanciful. 'Are you really going to live here?' he asked her dubiously.

'It's mine. Dulcie left it to me when she died three years ago.'

'A pity she didn't leave you any money to make it habitable.'

Miranda turned her head at that. 'I hadn't told her about the problems we were having at Fairchild's,' she said with a clear look. 'I'm sure she assumed that I would have plenty of money of my own. She left a fortune to the animal rescue centre, but she knew how much I loved it here, and I'll always be grateful to her for making Whitestones mine.'

She looked back at the sea. 'Everything started to go horribly wrong not long after she died. For a long time it was all I could do to keep things together at Fairchild's. My father was in a terrible state, and Belinda and Octavia simply didn't understand what was going on and why they couldn't keep their allowances. I had to sell everything that meant so much to them— the houses, the horses, the paintings, the cars...' Miranda sighed. 'It was a horrible time, and all through it the thought of Whitestones was all I had to hang onto. I can't explain what it meant to me.'

There was a faint crease between Rafe's brows. It sounded as if Miranda had had to deal with everything by herself. Why had her family let her take on that burden alone? She hadn't had an easy time of it, then or now.

'Did you never consider selling? At least then you wouldn't be spending your evenings as a waitress.'

She shrugged. 'I'm not sure it's worth that much. You've seen the condition it's in, and not many people would want to walk over the field to get to the house.'

'You could put in a track.'

'Maybe, but you would have to negotiate with the farmer. It would take ages and cost a lot of money. How many prospective purchasers could be bothered? And why should I sell it?' Her chin had a stubborn tilt that was already becoming familiar to Rafe. 'It was nothing to do with Fairchild's. It's the only thing that's ever been mine, and I'm not going to let it go.'

'So you're going to leave London to live all alone in a decrepit cottage miles from anywhere, without the most basic of conveniences, and run a business you haven't been able to think of yet?'

The chin went up a notch. 'I won't be all alone. I'm going to have a dog.'

'Miranda Fairchild, I can't believe you would even *think* of doing anything so reckless and impractical,' said Rafe, but his voice was warm with an unmistakable undercurrent of laughter.

'I know.'

She *did* know. Miranda turned her head back to look at Rafe and was gripped by a feeling of unreality. He really was impossibly handsome. He had no business looking that good.

It was hard to imagine anyone who belonged less at Whitestones than Rafe did right then, but Miranda was suddenly, desperately aware of him again. It was as if every cell in her body were tingling with the knowledge that he was *there*, sitting only inches away, close enough to touch.

In spite of looking so utterly out of place, he was relaxed, long legs drawn up on the steps, broad wrists dangling between his knees, and yet still exuding vitality and virility. Those big hands had held her as he waltzed her round the floor. His palm had been warm against her back, his clasp strong around her fingers.

The memory quivered in the pit of her stomach, and Miranda made herself look away. Not that it did much good. Not looking at his hands meant looking at the masculine, exciting lines of his face instead, at his jaw, his cheek, his chin. At the cool, humorous mouth with the heart-tugging curl at the corner, and her mouth promptly dried.

Feeling her gaze on him, Rafe turned his head to meet her gaze, and she was snared helplessly in the gleaming dark blue depths of his eyes, unable to look away as the oxygen was sucked from the air. Unable to breathe, Miranda was left dizzy, trembling, and yet exhilarated at the same time.

She had never felt like this before, never been so overwhelmed by the intensity of her senses. She could feel the roughness of the wooden step beneath her with a preternatural clarity, hear the sound of the sea on the shingle as she had never heard it before. The sun was warm like a caress on her arms,

and the salt tang of the air mingled with the scent of fresh grass
and bleached wood.

And of the lethally attractive man next to her, sitting there
with those wickedly glinting eyes and that mouth…oh, that
mouth! Rafe Knighton was way out of her league, Miranda
knew that, and yet right now it seemed utterly right that he
should be there, inexplicably bound up in the perfection of the
moment, and without warning she was seized by a wild happiness, so sharp and intense it was almost painful.

This moment was hers, and she would never forget it.

'I know,' she said again, not quite steadily. Tearing her eyes
from his at last, she laughed, still giddy with it. 'It's madness.'

'Complete madness,' Rafe agreed, but then he was laughing
too, and with a mixture of relief and regret Miranda felt the
terrible, wonderful intensity dissolve. 'I like the idea that you're
not always sensible and careful.'

'I am except when I'm here.'

'Then this is where you should be.'

Grateful to him for understanding, Miranda smiled at him
as she got to her feet. 'I'll show you the beach.'

They followed the coastal path a little way until it dipped
down to a stream, where they could clamber over the stones to
reach the empty beach that stretched back under the cliff
towards Whitestones. Gentle waves broke onto the shingle with
a whoosh and a rustle before they were sucked relentlessly
back into the sea.

A light breeze lifted their hair, teasing tendrils out of Miranda's
tight band. They blew around her face, tickling her cheek, so that
she had to keep lifting a hand to smooth them away. Their feet
crunched over the stones, but it was hard walking in heels.

Miranda muttered an exclamation of frustration at last.
'These shoes are hopeless for the beach,' she said, bending to
take them off. 'Turn your back a moment.'

'Why?'

'I want to take my tights off.'

'I'm certainly seeing a new side to you today,' he said, but he turned obediently away to pull off his own shoes and socks while Miranda wriggled awkwardly out of her tights.

Rolling up his trousers, Rafe followed her down to the narrow band of rough sand by the water, where it was easier to walk than on the uneven shingle.

'You'll get wet,' Miranda warned as the waves broke over their feet, and swirled around their ankles.

'You can't come to the seaside and not paddle.'

Rafe was enjoying the sight of the prim and proper Miranda Fairchild wandering barefoot along a beach, sensible shoes dangling from one hand, hair escaping at last from that horrible severe style she insisted on wearing, but when she turned to smile at him she looked so happy that his heart stumbled for a moment.

Just a moment, though. Rafe recovered so quickly that he almost managed to convince himself that it had never happened.

Almost.

'Won't you be lonely here on your own?' he asked her. 'And pets don't count!'

'I'd rather be lonely than with the wrong person,' said Miranda after a moment. 'I've seen what that's like.'

'Your parents?'

She nodded. 'I suppose they must have loved each other once, but I think the attraction they had for each other can only ever have been physical. Once that had worn off, they were just two strangers who didn't like each other very much, living in the same house. They used to fight all the time and throw recriminations at each other.'

Miranda hugged her arms together, the shoes still hooked over the fingers of one hand. 'My father would claim my mother had only married him for his money, which was partly true, and then she'd shout that he'd only wanted her for her title, which was also partly true. I think they must have liked fighting, actually. They were both very emotional and dramatic, so perhaps it satisfied some craving for attention, but it was exhausting for the rest of us. It was actually a relief when Mummy finally left.'

Rafe was surprised at how vividly he could picture Miranda as a small, too-restrained child, hating the constant drama and scenes her parents created around her. 'How old were you?'

'I was twelve, but Octavia was only eight. She was only a little girl. It was awful for her.'

Twelve wasn't very old to cope with losing your mother either, Rafe thought.

'It was hard for Belinda too,' Miranda added fairly, unaware of his mental interruption. 'Even though she was fourteen, she was closest to our mother, and she looks exactly like her. My father was terribly humiliated, but he put a good face on it and we soon got used to an ever-changing succession of girlfriends who all looked remarkably like our mother.'

Poor little kid, thought Rafe. He'd bet that, even at twelve, Miranda had been the one to look after her sisters. 'So you lived with him rather than your mother?'

'In theory. We'd go and stay with our mother sometimes, but it was never a great success. I think we made her feel old.' She smiled, but without much humour. 'Daddy did his best, but his idea of parenting was to send us to expensive schools, but not so that we could go on and get good jobs. It was to make sure we met all the best people and were invited to all the best parties, so that eventually we could marry just as he and our mother did and make all the same mistakes!'

Miranda shook her head, releasing more little tendrils from her ponytail. 'He was absolutely delighted when Belinda married Charles, mainly because Charles has a minor title.

They had the society wedding of the year. You'd probably have been invited if you'd been around,' she said with a sideways glance at Rafe, walking barefoot beside her and managing to look perfectly groomed with his trousers rolled up to his ankles.

'It cost an absolute fortune, but it was all worth it apparently,' she went on, unable to disguise the thread of bitterness in her voice. 'The wedding was featured in all the glossy magazines. Everyone said it was a great success, so I suppose it must have been. Never mind that it was the final straw that broke Fairchild's.'

She broke off a little guiltily. 'I'm sorry, that sounds like sour grapes, doesn't it? I ought to be happy for Belinda. She's happy, and that's what matters. She's got the perfect yummy-mummy lifestyle she always wanted, even if she does have to put up with Charles braying like a donkey whenever he laughs—

'There I go again,' she caught herself up once more. 'I was always being told how I would never get married unless I learnt to sweeten my tongue a bit, as if that was the worst thing that could ever happen to me! I ought to be nicer, but it was so frustrating to see my father spending money hand over fist when the company was in such trouble.'

'The company didn't pay for your sister's wedding, did it?'

'My father treated Fairchild's like a private bank account,' said Miranda bitterly. 'He thought it was there to provide him with the lifestyle he felt entitled to. He never thought about the people whose jobs depended on the company. Actually, I don't think he ever realised that everything he liked to do—eating out in the most expensive restaurants, buying the best wines, getting his shirts made in Jermyn Street, skiing in Gstaad, all that stuff—*all* of it was dependent on Fairchild's.'

Frustration churned in her still whenever she thought about it. 'I tried so hard to turn things round. Daddy couldn't be bothered with the business side of things, so he was happy to turn most of the day-to-day running of the company over to me, but as soon as Belinda announced her engagement it was hopeless. He was determined that she should have the best of everything.

'It was obscenely extravagant.' Miranda shuddered at the memory. 'I can't bear to think about it: the dress, the invitations, the flowers, the table decorations, the food, the champagne, the special entertainer for children… It was all so over the top.'

'Weddings often are excessive,' Rafe commented mildly.

'But why?' Miranda stopped and watched a tanker inch its way along the horizon. 'It seems to me that if you want to get married, you shouldn't need all that brouhaha. It should be about two people making a commitment to each other. You don't need five hundred guests and a flotilla of bridesmaids and pageboys for that.'

'You're very severe,' said Rafe, standing beside her. 'A wedding is the most important day of most people's lives. What's wrong with wanting to make it special?'

'Well, if I ever get married, it's going to be just me and a man who loves me,' said Miranda defiantly. 'All we'll need is each other. We'll have a simple ceremony, then we'll come here and sit on the beach when it's dark. Maybe we'll have some champagne and listen to the sea and just be together.'

'And then?'

'Then we'll go back to Whitestones and make love all night, and know that when we wake in the morning the sun will be streaming through the window, and we'll have the rest of our lives to spend together.'

'Miranda, you're a romantic!' Rafe's smile held more affection than mockery. 'I never expected that.'

Up went the chin in a gesture that already seemed heart-clenchingly familiar. 'You're not, I suppose?'

'I don't think I can be,' he confessed, 'but I can certainly see the appeal of your wedding. What will you be wearing?'

She stared at him, disconcerted by the abrupt question. 'What?'

'You seem to have imagined your wedding in some detail. I just wondered what you were going to wear to make the occasion special—or will you just be in one of your neat little grey suits?'

'Of course not,' said Miranda, but she hesitated. 'I don't know about a dress,' she admitted after a moment. 'I'm not very good at clothes.'

Rafe put his head on one side and considered her. 'I think you should wear something very simply designed, but in a soft, beautiful fabric. Something floaty, with chiffon perhaps, to make you look ethereal…like a mermaid.'

Miranda was embarrassed by how clearly she could imagine it as Rafe described her dress in his deep, warm voice. 'If I'm going to look like a mermaid, I should carry a bunch of seaweed perhaps?' she said in an attempt to puncture the sudden tension in the atmosphere.

'Meadow flowers would be better,' said Rafe, unfazed. 'And, of course, you'll have to let your hair down.' Without thinking, he reached out and pulled the band from her ponytail so that her hair slithered silkily forward. It was just as soft against his fingers as he had imagined, and he let out a careful breath.

Thrown ridiculously off balance by how she looked, standing there with the sun in her eyes and her hair spilling down to her shoulders, he made a great show of fluffing it up in a caricature of a hairdresser while he got his breathing under control.

'That's better,' he said.

Realising that she was trembling, Miranda snatched the band from his hands, and stepped back from the tantalising warmth of his hands.

'Thanks for the tip,' she said, hating the fact that her voice wasn't quite steady. 'If I ever get married, I'll certainly remember your advice.' She began walking along the sand again. 'I wouldn't hold your breath, though. I won't get married until I can find a man who is everything to me, a man who doesn't feel as if he's quite complete unless I'm beside him. I realise that may take a long time,' she added, hoping that she sounded wryly amused, but suspecting that instead she simply sounded wistful.

'Ah, so you're holding out for the fairy tale?'

Why couldn't *she* sound like that? Miranda wondered resentfully. That was exactly the tone she had hoped to achieve. 'It's that or nothing,' she said, glancing sideways to find him watching her with an indecipherable expression. 'I suppose you don't believe in fairy tales either?'

'No, I can't say I do,' said Rafe. 'I think that kind of all-encompassing love is overrated, to be honest. I'm not saying it doesn't exist. My parents had that kind of marriage. They were everything to each other, just the way you want to be with your husband.'

'You're lucky to have had that kind of model,' said Miranda, unable to keep the wistfulness from her voice this time.

'Maybe.' Rafe sounded unconvinced. 'From the outside, it always looks perfect. When my parents were together in a room you felt as if it was an effort for them to notice anyone else, even their own child. I always felt incidental to their marriage.'

'I'm sure they must have loved you,' Miranda said a little awkwardly.

'Oh, sure,' he said with a careless shrug. 'It wasn't as if I was neglected, or badly treated. Far from it. But I always knew that I wasn't necessary to them, not the way they were necessary to each other. It didn't seem to matter whether I was good or bad...so of course I was bad most of the time. Classic bid for attention, I'm afraid.'

He gave a short laugh that Miranda guessed was meant to be self-mocking, but which hinted instead at a small boy's bafflement and hurt at finding himself excluded from the intense relationship his parents shared.

'My father was shattered when my mother died,' Rafe went on. 'He never recovered from it. He withdrew into himself, became a workaholic, and, selfishly, I resented him for it. It's only recently that I've begun to wonder whether the reason he refused to give me any responsibility was because he was afraid to let go of anything to do with the company. Perhaps he thought that the moment he stopped working so hard he would have to face the emptiness of his life, and remember that without my mother he had nothing.'

'He had you.'

Rafe shook his head. 'I wasn't her. I was only fifteen and away at school. I never really had a chance to build a proper relationship with him. If they had been less bound up in each other, her death might have meant that we grew closer. As it was, I couldn't offer him any comfort.'

And his father had offered him none either. Miranda's heart twisted to realise how unhappy the wild, reckless boy Rafe had been.

By tacit consent, they had drifted to a halt once more and stood side by side, facing out to sea while the waves swooshed and swirled over their feet.

'If you don't want the fairy tale, what kind of marriage are you looking for?' she asked him after a moment.

Rafe didn't answer immediately. 'I'm not looking for an incredible love affair,' he said at last. 'I think if I was going to fall in love, I would have done it by now. I'm thirty-five, and I've known a lot of women. I've liked them and desired them, but I haven't *needed* them, and they haven't needed me either.'

'So who are you looking for at this ball when all these supposedly serious women turn up?'

Rafe was disconcerted to find that he couldn't think with her clear green eyes on him. How could he imagine his perfect bride when she was standing right there beside him? When he tried to picture the woman he would want to marry, all he got was Miranda's image, which was no help at all.

He had to be practical, after all. A wife who was determined to hide herself away in a place like this was obviously unsuitable. He needed someone who could be part of his life in London.

'Someone I like being with,' he decided in the end, conscious that it sounded a bit lame. 'Someone intelligent and cultured, with her own career and her own interests. I'd expect her to be sophisticated, I think, and capable of entertaining for me. And attractive,' he added honestly. 'Someone I could come to love without necessarily feeling a grand passion. The kind of relationship my parents had isn't healthy. If I have kids, I want them to feel part of things, not as if they're intruding.'

'Well, it shouldn't be too hard to find someone like that,' said Miranda, determinedly brisk. 'It's a lot easier if you're not looking for true love.'

'That's what I thought,' said Rafe, but suddenly it didn't seem as easy as it had before.

'I'd better get on with organising this ball, then.' Miranda produced a bright smile. 'Summer would be the best time. Everyone will be away in August, but we could try for mid or late July. What do you think?'

'The sooner the better as far as I'm concerned,' he said. 'It's May already, though. Do you think that'll be long enough for you to organise it?'

'It'll be tight,' she acknowledged, pulling her hair determinedly back into its ponytail. 'I'll just have to get on with it.' She glanced at Rafe as by unspoken consent they turned to make their way back down the beach to where he had left his shoes and socks. 'We'd better not have any more days like this for a while.'

Rafe watched her tie her hair back with a stupid pang of regret. He remembered how it had felt against his fingers, how the light had warmed it to dark honey, and made it gleam with gold. How Miranda had looked with the sea breeze tangling it around her face, her eyes dazzled by sun.

Why was he thinking about that? Rafe caught himself up. Really, it was high time he found himself a suitable bride, he decided. He wanted someone serious and serene and lovely, not prickly and impatient the way Miranda was. She wasn't beautiful. She *wasn't*.

And even if she had been perfect in every way, which she clearly wasn't, she was holding out for the fairy tale. For someone so practical, she was absurdly romantic, he thought. She seemed the last person to believe in true love.

Rafe scowled down at the sand. He couldn't imagine who Miranda would fall in love with. Obviously it would have to be someone insanely tidy, yet with no fashion sense, who didn't mind being slobbered over by dogs or walking across a sea of mud to live miles from anywhere without a single convenience.

No, she was right. There was no point in any more days like this. They were looking for completely different things. He needed to concentrate on finding someone suitable to settle down with, not on how Miranda looked walking straight-backed and slender beside him on the sand.

Rafe turned the car between the gates and into the welcome shade of the chestnut trees lining the avenue. It was a beautiful day, just as it had been when he first came here with Miranda. The ball had been just an idea then. It was hard to believe that it was happening tonight, and that tomorrow it would be over.

Miranda had been at Knighton Park for the past week, keeping an eagle eye on the preparations and making sure that

Elvira didn't have to deal with anything. He had had an email from her only that morning, reminding him to bring a present for his grandmother and to pick up the place cards, which had been sent back to the printer because they weren't exactly as she had ordered.

She had signed it simply 'Miranda'. No, 'love, M', no 'x' after her name. There were no exclamation marks or funny faces made with punctuation marks in Miranda's messages, which were unfailingly clear and crisp. Rafe knew that he ought to be grateful that she was so efficient and practical, but he couldn't help wishing sometimes that she would give some indication that he was more to her than just a boss.

He felt as if they had become unlikely friends over the past ten weeks, but it was hard to know exactly what Miranda herself thought. She had certainly done an incredible job of organising the ball in record time. Rafe had often seen her working late at her desk, and he'd fallen into the habit of stopping by to have a chat at the end of the day and see how plans were progressing.

He liked the cool detachment with which she viewed him, and the way she remained determinedly unimpressed by his looks or charm. He liked the humour in her clear green eyes, the irony that feathered her voice, the snippy comments that made him laugh. Miranda never tried to impress or flatter him, quite the opposite in fact. There was no danger of suffering from an inflated ego when she was around, he would grumble, but secretly he enjoyed being able to relax and be himself in a way he never seemed to be able to do with anyone else.

As the pace of the preparations had become more frantic Rafe had insisted that they spend every free lunchtime walking in Green Park.

'You can't waste the entire summer sitting in an office,' he told her when he discovered her working through her lunch hour one day. 'It's bad for you.'

'I haven't got time to go to the park,' objected Miranda.

Rafe tsk-tsked. 'You're just using work as an excuse. You know what I think the problem is? You're afraid!'

'Afraid?' she scoffed. 'Afraid of what?'

'Of enjoying yourself. I don't think you know how to relax and enjoy something simple like a walk in the sun,' he said provocatively.

'I'm perfectly capable of relaxing. I just don't have time with you interrupting every five minutes,' Miranda complained, but in the end she gave in and let Rafe bully her into getting up and going with him.

'Come on, stop grumbling, and if you're very good I'll buy you an ice cream,' he said with one of his slanting smiles.

The park quickly became part of their routine and Rafe found himself looking forward to it every day. He was disappointed if he had a lunchtime meeting and couldn't walk along the paths beside Miranda, straight-backed and composed and tart-tongued.

She would soften immediately when she saw a dog, though, and Rafe enjoyed watching the way her face lit up with a smile as she bent to greet them.

'That's torn it,' he would pretend to complain whenever he spotted a dog approaching, and he would roll his eyes exaggeratedly. 'Now we'll be here for half an hour while you make friends with yet another mutt!'

He always ended up talking to the owners while Miranda fussed over the dog, and he would watch her out of the corner of his eye, wishing that she would be that uninhibitedly affectionate with him. It had come to something when he was jealous of a dog!

'I don't know what you see in them,' he would grumble when the dog was eventually dragged away by its owner. 'They're such messy creatures. Look, you've got hairs all over your skirt.'

Miranda rolled her eyes as she brushed casually at her skirt. 'Honestly, I don't know how you can go on so much about *me* being repressed when you're so finicky.'

'I am not *finicky*!'

'Yes, you are. Look at the fuss you make about a few little hairs.'

'I don't like looking messy,' said Rafe a little defensively.

'Perhaps we should add fussy about their appearance to your list of attributes for an ideal bride,' Miranda suggested. 'Oh, I've got a good idea! Why don't I cull the invitation list? We should only invite obsessive compulsives on the grooming front and then you'd be bound to find a soul mate!'

'At least they would all care about their appearance, which is more than you do!' Rafe eyed her morosely. She persisted in wearing those dull grey skirts with a prim little top and sensible shoes, as if she had never heard of *colour*. She never wore make-up, never let her hair swing free, never made the slightest effort at all, in fact.

'Why do you always tie your hair back like that?' he grumbled.

'Because it's practical.'

'It would be prettier if you let it hang loose.'

'I don't do pretty,' said Miranda, unruffled. 'I leave that to my sisters.'

CHAPTER SIX

IT WAS true, of course. Miranda *wasn't* pretty, but the more Rafe looked at her, the more he noticed the fineness of her skin, the subtleness of her colouring, the clear, cool lines of her that plucked at a chord deep inside him, vibrating through him and making him itch with the longing to peel those awful clothes off her, to run his fingers through her hair and explore her, unlock her, with his mouth and his hands. Making him imagine what it would be like to warm her and excite her and drive her to a pitch of passion where she would lose her primness and reveal the warm, vibrant woman he was convinced lurked beneath her deliberately dull façade.

But of course he couldn't do that. Miranda had made it very clear that she wasn't interested in him. And he wasn't interested in *her*, Rafe told himself. Not really.

He reminded himself of his plan. It had made such good sense when he first thought about getting married, and it still *did* make sense. All he needed was to find the right woman, and then he wouldn't feel this restless and edgy and dissatisfied. He wouldn't be distracted by fantasies about a plain, prim girl who preferred dogs to men and had a totally impractical plan to live in the middle of nowhere without the most basic of amenities.

It would be such a relief to find the right woman and settle down. She would steady him and help him focus. Everyone would take him seriously. He would *be* serious.

Rafe couldn't wait.

All he had to do was find her. Until the ball, there was no point in giving up an active social life. You never knew who you were going to meet. So Rafe went to dinner parties and cocktail parties and champagne receptions and fund raising events. He went to Wimbledon and Ascot and the Henley regatta. He went everywhere he was invited in the hope of encountering his perfect woman.

He was at a gallery opening one evening when he spotted an attractive blonde studying one of the paintings with an intense expression. Rafe's hopes rose. She was very stylishly dressed, and looked just his type.

Her name was Rachel, he discovered when he introduced himself, and they talked about the picture for a while. Close up, she was even more attractive. Could Rachel be the one he was waiting for? She was beautiful, intelligent, sophisticated. She was perfect.

So why could he feel boredom stealing over him?

What was wrong with him? Rafe wondered in frustration, redoubling his efforts to be charming. Rachel was exactly the kind of woman he was looking for.

She blossomed visibly under his attention, and he willed himself to be captivated, concentrating hard on her face until he saw her wave somebody away with a dismissive hand. The gesture caught his attention more than what she was saying and he turned, only to find himself staring straight into Miranda's clear green eyes.

Jolted, even jarred, by the sight of her, Rafe couldn't tear his gaze away. Unmasked tonight, she was demurely dressed in black. Her hair was neatly tied back and her face as bare as ever, and he felt the by now familiar spurt of irritation that she made so little effort to make the most of herself.

'Would you like a canapé?' she asked him, deadpan, but her eyes gleamed with irony.

Rachel shook her head, evidently cross at having her tête-à-tête with Rafe interrupted, but he pretended to inspect the tray Miranda held.

'What are these?' he asked, pointing.

'Chicken satay,' said Miranda.

'Are they good?'

'Everything's good,' she said.

Rachel was clearly baffled by the attention Rafe was paying a mere waitress, and looked at Miranda with incomprehension.

'No, thank you,' she said with emphasis when Miranda offered her tray once more.

Miranda took the hint and moved off.

Rafe was unaware that he was looking after her until Rachel put her hand on his arm to reclaim his attention.

'They will try and shove food down your throat at these events,' she complained.

Rafe didn't answer. He tried to concentrate on the conversation, but part of him was acutely aware of Miranda moving round the room with her tray, slender and unobtrusive in black.

It was amazing how nobody else seemed to notice her. Their eyes might pass incuriously over her, but they didn't see her at all. Rafe marvelled that no one registered how fine her features were, how clear her gaze. They had no idea how prickly and stubborn she could be, obviously.

They had no idea how a smile lit up her face, how light she felt in his arms. They didn't know that her hair was like silk and smelt like a summer afternoon, or how sharp and funny she could be.

It gave Rafe a strange thrill of possession to realise that he was the only person in the room to know those things about Miranda. Out of the corner of his eye, he watched her circulating with her tray and remembered her dancing in the dusty ballroom, bending down to greet every passing dog in the park. He remembered her tsk of impatience as she rubbed a mark off his sleeve, the way she rolled her eyes at him, or sat primly behind her desk.

And then he remembered how she had looked in that cat suit, and promptly wished he hadn't. It was criminal the way she kept those lovely legs hidden away. The way she kept that hair scraped back from her face.

All at once Rafe had an image of Miranda at the beach, her hair blowing gold and honey around her face, and he drew a sharp breath.

'Rafe? Are you OK?'

'Er, yes, fine,' he said, realising belatedly that he hadn't been listening to a word Rachel had been saying. 'I'm sorry, I didn't catch that.'

This was no way to go about finding a wife.

But tonight would be different, Rafe resolved as the car crunched to a halt outside Knighton Park. He was bound to meet someone special tonight, and his search would be over at last.

Miranda would spend a few days sorting things out in the aftermath of the ball, and then she would move on to a new assignment. She wouldn't be in the office to distract him any more. There would be no more walks in the park, no more sessions with his feet propped on her desk, no more crisp emails without even the hint of an 'x' at the end.

He was being ridiculous, Rafe admonished himself, shutting the car door behind him with unnecessary emphasis. They had been planning this ball for ten weeks now. Tonight he would meet an array of intelligent, successful, interesting women, and with any luck would find that special one with whom he could settle down and spend the rest of his life.

What more did he want?

Miranda walked through the ballroom, clipboard in hand. Everything was ready.

The room had been cleaned until everything gleamed, and it looked wonderful. The floor was polished, the chandeliers glittered, and the glass sparkled. There were dramatic flower arrangements strategically placed around the room and the long windows stood open onto the terrace. Even the weather had obliged with perfect, soft summer days that had left the gardens looking at their best.

A huge marquee had been set up on the lawn beneath the terrace, and even now the round tables were being laid for the dinner. Rosie had been thrilled to take on the catering, but it was a big job, and she was frantically at work in the kitchens while worrying about whether the new waiters and waitresses drafted in would turn up on time.

'I wish you could do it,' she grumbled to Miranda. 'I know I can trust you.'

But Miranda had decided that she would have to be available in case of last minute crises. Any number of things might go wrong at the last minute, she thought, obsessively checking her list. She would lurk in the background and be ready to deal with any of them.

She had been at Knighton Park all week, overseeing the cleaning and the deliveries and the erection of the marquee and all the other myriad preparations that needed to be made. Although it had been hectic, it had been one of the happiest weeks she had spent since staying at Whitestones with Dulcie. She had struck up a real friendship with Elvira Knighton, whose sharp tongue and cackle reminded her often of her beloved godmother. They played Scrabble together in the evenings, and every afternoon Miranda walked Elvira's dogs and felt herself relax away from London's noise and crowds. She even caught herself wishing that the ball weren't happening. She didn't want anyone else coming to spoil her peace.

But coming they were. The ball had sold out quickly, although Miranda did wonder how many of those who were coming would have done so if they had had any inkling of Rafe's real purpose in inviting them to take a table. But she had made sure the invitations were cleverly designed and had targeted them carefully, and she was gratified that her strategy seemed to have worked. Rafe should be pleased with the range of guests who were coming tonight, from a sprinkling of starry celebrities to the most earnest of development workers. If nothing else, it should be an interesting mix.

Once word had got out that it was by Rafe's invitation only, the Knighton Park ball had become the hottest ticket in town, and Belinda was still sulking because Miranda and Octavia would be there and not her.

'Charles would have bought a table,' she had complained. 'Why didn't you ask us?'

Miranda didn't want to say that Belinda and Charles hardly fell into the category of the kind of people Rafe wanted to meet, so she murmured something evasive about limited numbers.

'Then how did Octavia get an invite?'

'She's been working on the ball.'

Belinda snorted. 'Octavia? Octavia never worked in her life!' Which was pretty good coming from Belinda.

Once she'd heard about the ball, of course, Octavia had been wild to come, and had badgered Miranda relentlessly to get her a ticket.

'Just one dance with Rafe,' she had pleaded. 'That's all I need.'

Miranda could have told her sister that Rafe was looking to share his fortune with a very different kind of woman, but in the end she had agreed on the condition that she helped out with organising the ball. Whatever else Octavia was, she had a real sense of style, and some of her suggestions had been very useful. Miranda had been hoping that her sister would get used to the idea of a job, as she had explained to her ex-boss Simon when asking if she could draft in Octavia in some capacity.

Simon had agreed to give Octavia a temporary position, but Miranda's plan to introduce her little sister to a working life could not be said to have been an unqualified success. Octavia had certainly declared her willingness to advise on stylistic issues, but this hadn't translated into turning up at the office at agreed times, or staying any longer than it suited her.

'I had to have highlights done,' she explained artlessly when Miranda tackled her. She tossed back the blonde hair in question. 'Anyway, I was bored. Simon just sits there and looks disapproving. Doesn't he ever smile?'

'He's busy.'

'Well, it wouldn't hurt him to lighten up a bit, would it?'

It was a pity Simon had to be the one man in the world resistant to Octavia's beauty, Miranda reflected. He was just what she needed. He was kind and steady and reliable, but strong enough not to put up with any of her sister's nonsense. He would make a wonderful husband.

Unlike Rafe, for instance, whose life out of the office still seemed to be given over to amusement as far as Miranda could make out. Every week he was in the celebrity magazines, photographed at one social event or another. If he was trying to make people believe that he was a serious person now, he was going about it in a very strange way.

The trouble was, he just *wasn't* serious. He had one of those faces that always looked as if they were about to break into a smile, and his eyes danced with humour even when he was at his most straight-faced.

No man ought to have that much charm at his disposal, Miranda often thought. It was positively wicked. But there was something about his presence that put a fizz in the air and a tingle in the blood, that made her senses sharpen and laughter bubble in her throat, although she tried never to show it.

Miranda would rather stick pins in her eyes than admit it, but she had missed Rafe this week. The truth was that she had got used to seeing him every day, lounging with feet up on her desk, or forcing her to spend her lunch hour in the park. She missed his glinting smile. She missed his teasing. She missed arguing with him and eating ice cream with him and laughing with him. She even missed the finickity way he brushed dog hairs from his trousers.

She wasn't a fool. Miranda knew how little it would take for her to fall in love with him, and whenever she found herself slipping that way she would make herself take a long, hard look in the mirror.

You're plain, you're dull, you're *efficient*, she told herself bitterly. How likely is it that Britain's most eligible bachelor would fall for *you*?

Not likely at all.

In fact, it was hard to think of anything *less* likely to happen.

That way Rafe had of making you feel you were the only person in the world he really wanted to be with was just part of his charm. Miranda had seen him at social events when she was a waitress, having exactly the same effect on any number of gorgeously stylish and beautiful women, all of whom would fit perfectly into his life.

Unlike her.

No, Miranda had no intention of making a fool of herself. Rafe might have mocked her as a romantic, but in his case she couldn't afford not to be realistic. She was keeping a very careful guard on her heart.

This was just a job, she reminded herself endlessly. She was here to organise the ball, and when it was over she would find another job and that would be that. Rafe would marry someone serious and suitable and she...she would keep thinking about Whitestones.

Somewhere in the distance Miranda could hear Elvira's dogs break into a frenzy of barking. Was that Rafe arriving already? In spite of her sternest resolutions, Miranda's heart began to pound at the thought and, furious with herself, she drew a deep, steadying breath.

It didn't matter if Rafe was here or not. She had a job to do. And that was what she would do.

Taking a firm grip of herself, Miranda marched briskly out onto the terrace and then down the steps to see how they were getting on in the marquee. She could put the seating plans up.

The entrance to the marquee was pulled right back to let in the air, but it still smelt of hot tent and flowers inside. The tables looked wonderful and Miranda walked round them, checking each last detail, pleased with the result of all her planning. There was a subdued murmur of voices in the catering area, but it didn't sound as if there was any crisis, so she decided to leave Rosie to it.

A discreet board had been set up near the entrance, and she was pinning up the seating plan when Rafe found her.

'So this is where you are! I've been looking all over for you.'

Immediately, what little air there was in the marquee evaporated. Miranda felt as if a fist had closed around her heart. Furious to find that her hands were shaking slightly, she pinned up the last plan and turned to face him.

'Hello.'

Her voice was quite steady, which was surprising when she felt heady with the intensified scents around her, the smell of the canvas mingling with the cut grass outside. Or maybe it was just Rafe's presence, the smile in his eyes and the crease in his cheeks and those impossibly white teeth, that was making her dizzy. Or the fierce joy that had speared through her at the sound of his voice.

'Hello,' he returned, and then seemed to run out of anything to say.

There was a pause, which stretched into an uncomfortable silence. Miranda knew she should make a cool comment, but the tension in the air was making her heart thump, and her mind was blank of anything other than the terrifying awareness of Rafe, so that all she could do was stand there dumbly and stare back into the dark blue eyes where the usual glinting smile had been replaced by a disconcerted expression that must have matched her own.

It felt as if they stood staring at each other for ages, but when Miranda thought about it sensibly afterwards, she realised it could only have been a few seconds before Rafe looked away and broke the silence.

'What are you doing?'

'The seating plan.'

To Miranda's dismay, Rafe moved over to stand right next to her and study the board.

'We agreed all this last week,' she reminded him, edging away as unobtrusively as possible.

'I've forgotten,' said Rafe. 'Where am I sitting, again?'

So then she had to move back to point his place out to him. 'I've put you between a human rights lawyer and a consultant for the World Bank,' she told him.

'Hmm.' Rafe looked at the names of the two women Miranda had decided made the most likely partners for him. She had done exactly what he had asked her to. So why did he feel so disgruntled about it? 'And where are you?'

'I'm not eating.'

'Why not?'

'Because I'm not a guest,' she said, wondering why she needed to state the obvious. 'I'm working.'

'There's no rule that says you can't eat while you're working, is there?'

'I need to be on hand to keep an eye on things,' Miranda told him, recovering her balance somewhat. 'Something's bound to go wrong at the last minute.'

'You're going to come and dance, though, aren't you?'

'I won't know anyone.'

'You'll know me.'

'You'll be busy getting to know all these women I've invited for you to meet,' she pointed out as crisply as she could. 'Besides, I haven't got anything to wear. I'll stay behind the scenes.'

On the surface she seemed steady enough, Miranda hoped, but she could feel the precariousness of her control. All Rafe had to do was take a step nearer, or smile at her, or touch her, and it would shatter completely. She was desperate to get away and compose herself.

From somewhere she produced a brilliant smile. 'Now, if you'll excuse me, I've still got a lot to do.'

She hurried away and for the rest of the afternoon kept herself too busy to think about how pathetically she had reacted to Rafe's appearance. At half past six, she calculated that she just had time for a shower before flinging on a black shirt and a clean pair of black trousers. Quickly drying her hair, she brushed it back and secured it with a scrunchie. There, now she was perfectly dressed to fade into the background, Miranda thought with satisfaction. She looked neat and businesslike and unobtrusive, just the way she liked it.

Before heading down to check that all was under control in the marquee, she made her way along to Elvira's sitting room.

Rafe had tried to persuade his grandmother to go to the ball, but she had laughed and told him not to be so silly.

'The last thing you want is an old lady like me there,' she said trenchantly. 'Besides I'm too old for all that. I won't hear anything on this side of the house, so I'll go to bed early and hear all about it in the morning.'

Miranda put her head round the sitting room door. 'Is there anything you need before we start?' Much to her relief, Rafe wasn't there.

'Come in and let me have a look at you,' his grandmother ordered, but her face changed as Miranda advanced into the room.

'What on *earth* are you wearing?' she demanded.

Miranda looked down at herself. 'Er...black.'

'You can't go to a ball dressed like that!'

'I'm not going to a ball,' said Miranda. 'I'm strictly back-stage tonight.'

'You most certainly are not! Go and put on a dress.'

'I haven't got anything with me,' she tried to explain, and Elvira heaved herself out of her chair with a dramatic sigh.

'You're about as stubborn as that grandson of mine. Come with me.'

Ignoring Miranda's protests that she had things to do, Elvira led the way to a dressing room with a whole wall of wardrobes. She flung open the doors and began rifling through the now-vintage designer dresses that had been carefully hung in covers.

'You're about the size I was when I was young, and I've never thrown anything away. I wonder if...' She pulled out a hanger and peered at the outfit. 'Maybe.' Flinging it at Miranda, she carried on, tossing the occasional outfit into Miranda's hapless arms until at last she drew a satisfied breath.

'*This* is the one,' she said. 'Put all those down and try this on.'

'B-but I can't wear your dress,' Miranda stammered, but Elvira refused to listen.

'Put it on,' she ordered.

Helplessly, Miranda found herself stripping down to her pants and stepping into the dress. A strapless sheath, it was exquisitely cut, with a row of tiny covered buttons that Elvira did up with surprisingly deft fingers, all the way down to the small of her back. It fit snugly under the bust with a ribbon effect, and then curved over her hips and down in a tulip shape before finishing in a stylish fishtail.

'Much better,' said Elvira with satisfaction. 'That's the perfect colour for you.'

In spite of her awkwardness, Miranda couldn't resist smoothing down the shot silk. 'It's a lovely green.'

'That's not just green. It's *greengage*. I had it made specially for me in London just after I got married. What a summer that was!' Elvira's keen eyes softened reminiscently before she recollected herself. 'Of course, I wore long gloves with it, but you won't want those on a hot night like this.'

'Elvira, it's terribly generous of you, but I really can't wear this,' Miranda tried again, wondering how on earth she would ever get those buttons undone. An image of Rafe slowly unbuttoning her with long, warm fingers flashed into her mind, and her breath stumbled at the thought before she pushed it firmly away.

'You'll hurt me very much if you refuse,' said Elvira, who, as Rafe had once pointed out, was not above emotional blackmail when it suited her. 'Of course, if you'd rather not…' she went on, assuming the air of a decrepit and tearful old lady that had Miranda stammering an acceptance even though she knew perfectly well that Elvira was putting it on.

'That's agreed, then,' said Elvira, miraculously restored to vigour. 'I suppose it's too much to hope that you'd have the same size shoes. You certainly can't wear *those*,' she added, wincing at the sight of Miranda's sensible flatties.

She looked through what seemed like racks and racks of

shoes and eventually selected a pair of elegantly strappy sandals. 'You might be able to get away with these.'

Surrendering to a force greater than herself, Miranda tried them on. 'They're a bit tight,' she said, making a face as she wriggled her toes.

'They'll do fine,' said Elvira. 'You must be prepared to suffer for beauty. Now, all you need is to do something about your hair and put on some lipstick. In my day I wouldn't have dreamed of going out in the evening without so much as a dab of make-up. You girls don't have standards any more.'

Miranda was desperate by now to get downstairs and make sure everything was ready. She would find some lipstick if she had a moment, but there were more important things to do first.

She bent to kiss Elvira's cheek. 'Thank you,' she said, touched by Rafe's grandmother's generosity even while she wondered how on earth she was going to get through the evening feeling half-naked. She even found herself thinking fondly of the catsuit. It might have clung in an embarrassingly revealing way, but at least she hadn't had all this flesh on display then. She would have to try and find a cardigan or a pashmina or something to cover her bare back and shoulders.

'Off you go,' said Elvira briskly. 'And don't hide yourself away all evening!'

Determined to do just that, Miranda hurried down the magnificent staircase, only to find herself face to face with Octavia in the hall.

'Are you here already?' she asked, surprised. 'I thought you were coming down with Cassandra and the Fox-Smythes?'

Very faint colour touched her sister's lovely cheeks. 'Simon offered me a lift,' she said a little too airily, 'so I thought I might as well come with him and—' Octavia broke off, as if noticing Miranda's appearance for the first time. 'You look fantastic!'

she said in surprise. 'Where did you get that *fabulous* dress?' she added enviously.

'Rafe's grandmother insisted I wear it.' Miranda fiddled fretfully with the plunging neckline. 'I can't hurt her feelings by taking it off, but I feel half-naked!'

'That's because you've got no make-up on.'

'Don't *you* start! I haven't got time for make-up. I've got to check that Rosie is OK.'

'Rosie's fine,' said Octavia and took her sister firmly by the arm. 'The last thing she needs is you fussing around. You're not ruining that dress by going out with nothing on your face.'

Miranda rolled her eyes. 'Oh, for heaven's sake!'

But Octavia was serious, and not taking no for an answer. She bore Miranda off to her bedroom and opened her bag. 'Now sit still,' she ordered.

Miranda hardly recognised herself when Octavia had finished. She stared at her reflection in something like shock. Was that really her, with her hair swinging shining to her bare shoulders? With those eyes, the ones she had always thought of as ditchwater dull, now cunningly emphasised so that they looked huge and brilliantly green? With that mouth, outlined in a colour that Octavia informed her, apparently quite seriously, was called Passionate Encounter. It made her look warm and sophisticated and really quite sexy, all at the same time.

She swallowed.

'*Now* can you see why we keep going on at you to make more of an effort?' demanded Octavia. 'You've never had any idea how beautiful you are.'

'But this isn't me,' said Miranda in a small voice.

'It *is* you,' said Octavia, exasperated. 'Or it's how you could be if only you'd have some confidence in yourself.'

Miranda didn't believe her, but she didn't want to get into

an argument about it. 'It's very clever, what you've done,' she said placatingly instead.

'Yes, well, I'm not just a pretty face, you know. Off you go now,' Octavia added in almost exactly the same tone Elvira had used. 'I want to get ready myself.'

Thanking her a little lamely, Miranda made her way to the ballroom. She felt very strange. She kept catching glimpses of an elegant stranger in the mirrors and realising with a belated shock that it was *her*. Between them, Elvira and Octavia had transformed her. Miranda just wished that they had changed her inside too, while they were at it. As it was, she felt exposed and vulnerable, and wished that her clipboard were three times the size so that she could hide all her bare flesh behind it.

Lurking as unobtrusively as she could, and keeping the clipboard clutched firmly in front of her, Miranda waited in the hall to direct guests out to the marquee as they arrived. Much to her relief, she hadn't seen Rafe at all. He must be in the marquee.

Only when she was sure that she was in no danger of being noticed in the crowd did Miranda make her own way there. The marquee was unrecognisable from the hot, quiet space where she and Rafe had stared at each other earlier. Now it was thronging with brightly dressed guests and the noise level was deafening.

Keeping to the edges, Miranda kept an eye on the tables until the guests were all sitting down and the first course was under way. She was determined not to look for Rafe, but she knew where he was sitting, of course, and it was impossible not to notice him. He was sitting between a vivacious brunette and a coolly beautiful blonde, but it was impossible to tell which was the lawyer and which the financial consultant. Rafe was smiling, exuding his usual charm and dividing his attention between them. Miranda couldn't tell which one he seemed more interested in—and she didn't care, she reminded herself quickly, turning away.

Now that the dinner was under control, she should be checking the band had everything it needed to set up in the ballroom, anyway.

The music started after the main course, and gradually dancers drifted up to the ballroom from the marquee, exclaiming at how beautiful it was. Miranda observed the floor fill up from her position in a quiet doorway. The band was fantastic and the floor was soon packed. She saw Octavia dancing with Simon. She saw Rafe dancing with a succession of lovely girls and apparently enjoying himself immensely.

Good, Miranda thought.

To her embarrassment, men kept asking her to dance. 'I'm sorry, I'm working,' she would have to explain, lifting her clipboard to underline the point. If only she could have stayed in her black trousers nobody would be making this mistake. Her feet in Elvira's shoes were killing her too.

The evening wore on. The meal was eaten, the champagne drunk, the dances danced. It had all gone like clockwork. Only another hour or so and it would be over.

Trying to ignore her sore feet, Miranda watched everyone enjoying themselves and willed herself to feel excited, or proud at least. She had made this happen, after all, and it was clearly a huge success. She could put it on her CV, and perhaps it would help her to find a job. She would have to go back to the agency and see if they had a new assignment for her. Rafe didn't need her any more. If he couldn't find a suitable wife among this lot, there was no hope for him.

Without thinking, she sought Rafe through the crowd. He was dancing with yet another girl, another blonde, who looked vaguely familiar. He might have danced with her before, so a second dance might mean that he was interested? When he smiled down into her eyes like that, was he thinking that she was the one?

Miranda turned away, suddenly overwhelmed by tiredness and melancholy, and slipped out to the terrace. There was no more she could do now, in any case. She could go off duty, surely. Her feet couldn't stand another second in these shoes.

Her heart couldn't stand another second pretending it didn't hurt just as much.

The night was warm, and the music spilled out over the paving. Taking off her shoes, Miranda went down the steps and with a sigh of relief curled her bare toes into the cool grass. A little further along the path, a stone bench was hidden in the shadows, and she sank down onto it, lips pressed together in a fierce line to stop the tears that clogged the back of her throat.

She was just tired, Miranda tried to convince herself. It was just anticlimax, just sore feet. Otherwise she wouldn't be feeling so pathetic.

Everything was *fine*. She had successfully completed an interesting project, and, with all the overtime and evening work, she had managed to save more than usual recently. True, she was still a long way from her target, but if she kept working it might not be too long before she could go to Whitestones and be happy.

What more did she want?

CHAPTER SEVEN

MIRANDA'S mind flickered to Rafe, but she clamped down immediately on the thought. Oh, for heaven's sake! she told herself, exasperated. Don't be so *silly*.

She sat on in the darkness, watching the stars that spangled the deep, dark blue of the sky. She could still hear the band and the sound of laughter from the ballroom but it was muted here, and, enveloped in the scents of the summer night, Miranda gradually relaxed. Everything *was* fine, she thought, and this time she meant it.

She was fine.

Even when a familiar figure materialised out of the shadows, she kept her calm, and if a flush crept into her cheeks, well, he wouldn't be able to see much in the darkness. He wouldn't see her heart pounding or the tingle of awareness beneath her skin.

Rafe stopped in front of her. 'What are you doing sitting out here in the dark, Miranda?'

'Resting my feet.'

Her bare shoulders were luminous in the starlight, and in that elegant dress she looked like a stranger, but the tilt of her chin and the directness of her gaze were unmistakably Miranda's.

Rafe's head was reeling. All evening, he had been keeping an eye out for Miranda, and getting increasingly frustrated at her absence, until quite suddenly he had spotted her, although he had had to look twice to make sure that it was really her.

He had never seen her look like that before. It was impossible not to recognise the trademark proud lift of her chin, the straight back and prim posture, and of course she had that damned clipboard held in front of her like a shield. There was no mistaking that.

But he was shaken to see her in a dress that clung lovingly to her figure and showed off her beautiful skin. The dress was old-fashioned, but it suited her somehow. It was unique, like Miranda herself. In it she looked elegant and ethereal, and quite unlike the frumpy assistant he was used to seeing.

She looked beautiful.

And once Rafe had seen her, he couldn't help seeing her everywhere. He tried not to stare, but he was aware of her all the time, and every time he saw another man approach her he felt himself tense, hoping that she wouldn't agree to dance. It made him furious to realise that he wasn't the only man who had noticed her.

When Miranda had slipped out onto the terrace, Rafe had seen her go. He'd told himself not to follow her. He was supposed to be having a good time. He was supposed to be finding a suitable wife.

So he'd kept on dancing, and when that dance had ended, he'd taken his partner back to the table and asked someone else to dance. Like everyone else he had danced with, she had been witty and intelligent and attractive, but the ballroom had felt hot and airless and noisy, and once the dance was over and she had been escorted back to the table in her turn, Rafe had murmured an excuse and escaped outside, the way he had been wanting to do ever since Miranda had disappeared.

At first, he hadn't been able to see her anywhere, and, feeling a fool, he'd been about to head back to the ballroom when he had caught a glimpse of movement in the shadows. Now he looked down at her, sitting alone in the dark, the clipboard resting in her lap, and he could feel his heart swelling at the sight of her.

'Come and dance, Cinderella,' he said. 'You've been working all evening.'

'You're supposed to be dancing with your guests,' said Miranda, bracing herself to resist him. It wasn't fair of him to stand there, looking like that, *smiling* like that.

'I have danced with them,' said Rafe. 'I've been dancing all night, and now I want to dance with you,'

'Why?'

Yes, *why*? Rafe asked himself. He didn't know himself, he just knew that he did.

'To say thank you,' he improvised. 'You've done a fantastic job. Everybody's saying what a success the ball is, and you should be sharing in that, not hiding out here.'

'I'm not *hiding*. I'm tired, and my feet are killing me.' She showed him her bare feet. 'There's no way I'm putting those shoes on again!'

'Dance barefoot,' Rafe told her. 'But dance you will.' Reaching down, he took hold of her hand and tugged her, still protesting, to her feet. 'And you can leave that bloody thing here,' he added, removing the clipboard from her clutch and tossing it onto the bench. 'You don't need it any more.'

His grip warm and firm around her hand, he pulled Miranda up the steps and across the terrace, ignoring her attempts to hang back.

'You know, you could just say thank you,' she said breathlessly as she was dragged along. 'Or send me flowers tomorrow. I'd be fine with that. Or even better, a bonus!'

Rafe stopped suddenly just outside the doors, but didn't let go of her hand. 'Why don't you want to dance with me?' he demanded.

Miranda stared at him in frustration. She couldn't tell him that she didn't trust herself near him, that she was afraid of the way her body reacted to his closeness.

'I can't dance,' she muttered. 'You know that.'

'We danced before,' Rafe pointed out.

'That wasn't really dancing. And it wasn't in public.'

'Nobody's going to be interested in you, Miranda,' he tutted. 'It's not a display. Anyway, it's not even proper dancing. It's not as if we're going to do a formal waltz. Listen.'

It was very late, and the band had switched to slow music by now. 'See?' Rafe said. 'We don't need to dance at all. We just need to hold each other and sway a bit.'

That was what she was afraid of.

'Oh, well, if you're going to make such a fuss about it,' said Miranda, covering her nervousness beneath a familiar prickly manner. 'But I'd really rather have a bonus!'

Rafe laughed and pulled her onto the floor. 'I love it when you're charming, Miranda!'

As he had promised, no one was dancing properly. The floor was so crowded, they had little choice but to stand close together. Rafe curled his fingers firmly around hers and held her hand against his shoulder. He spread his other hand against the small of her back, feeling her stiff and rigid, and eased her nearer to him so that he could breathe in the scent of her hair.

This was what he had wanted to do all evening, he realised. He had danced with an array of women far more beautiful and sophisticated, but Miranda was the one he wanted.

It was madness, Rafe told himself. She was completely unsuitable for him in every way. They were totally incompatible. She didn't want him, didn't approve of him, and she had made it very clear that theirs was a strictly working relationship. It would be deeply inappropriate to suggest anything else.

So he couldn't let his lips drift over the silky hair, couldn't nudge it aside to kiss his way down her temple, couldn't nuzzle the warm, sweet pulse beneath her ear. Couldn't undo those little buttons down her back one by one and slide the dress off her so that he could make love to her.

Rafe felt his blood surge at the thought. What would it be like to unlock the tension in her, to get past those defensive barbs to the warm, vibrant woman he was so sure lurked beneath that prim exterior? To make her shudder with pleasure, to give her joy, to show her what fun there was in loving and being loved?

But Miranda wouldn't think an affair was fun, Rafe realised. She had told him that she was holding out for true love. She was dreaming of the fairy tale, not fun.

And he was no Prince Charming. He couldn't give her the fairy tale she wanted, and anything else would hurt her. That was the last thing he wanted to do.

No, this was one impulse he had to resist. Thanks to Miranda's organisation, he had met lots of interesting, attractive women tonight. His pocket was bulging with business cards, telephone numbers and email addresses. Any one of them might be the woman he was looking for.

Tomorrow he would start his quest to find her, Rafe vowed. But in the meantime, Miranda was warm and slender in his arms, and although he knew he shouldn't really be pulling her tighter, he couldn't resist doing it anyway. She was here for now. He would make the most of that.

'You look wonderful in that dress,' he told her.

'Your grandmother insisted I wear it.'

'Elvira always had taste. It's exactly the colour of your eyes.'

She looked up in surprise at that. 'No, it's not. Elvira said it was greengage.'

'So are your eyes.'

Miranda smiled uncertainly, as if unsure whether he was

joking or not. 'I've never thought of my eyes as green. They always look a murky ditchwater colour to me.'

'They're not murky at all,' said Rafe without thinking. 'They're the clearest eyes I've ever seen.'

She opened her mouth, but no words came out, and after a moment Rafe smiled and drew her close, shutting out everyone else in the ballroom as they danced in silence.

It was just as well Rafe made no attempt at conversation because Miranda couldn't have strung a sentence coherently together if she had tried. Her eyes were level with Rafe's crisp white collar and she was woozy with his nearness. She could feel his hand warm and insistent on her back. His other palm was pressed against hers, their fingers entwined, as he clasped her hand to his chest.

She tried to hold herself away from him, but it was hopeless. He was too solid, too warm, his body too inviting. Miranda scowled at his collar and concentrated on all the reasons why she shouldn't find Rafe attractive, but the more she thought about it, the more aware she was of him.

Out of the corner of her eye she could see the firm line of his jaw and the corner of that mouth. He wasn't smiling, but there was a dent in his cheek and a quirk to the set of his lips that sent warmth shivering through her. She tried looking away and staring at his jacket instead, but the material seemed to shimmer in front of her gaze after a while and her eyes slid surreptitiously back to his mouth.

It was so close. All he had to do was turn his head just a little and if she turned hers too, their lips would meet. What would that be like? The answer came in the leap of her heart, the acceleration of her pulse at the very thought, and Miranda closed her eyes against the instinctive knowledge of how thrilling it would be to touch her lips to his, to feel his mouth take sure, seductive possession of hers.

He would be a very good kisser. He had had lots of practice, after all. Miranda dragged the feverish drift of her thoughts back to reality. What was she thinking? That Rafe Knighton, playboy extraordinaire, would actually think about kissing *her*? He had his pick of beautiful women. Was it really likely that he would pass them all over in favour of plain Miranda Fairchild?

Miranda swallowed, embarrassed that she could have let herself even imagine it. She had had years to get used to being the plain sister, the one nobody noticed. It had been uncomfortable this evening feeling that everyone was looking at her, as if she were a little girl dressed up as someone else.

Which she was.

She was dressed as a beautiful, sophisticated woman instead of the prickly, plain girl she really was. It had been a mistake. If she had been wearing black trousers and sensible shoes, she wouldn't be here fighting temptation, torn between resistance and the yearning to lean against him and turn her face to his throat, to press her lips to his skin, and lose herself in the warm, solid safety of his body.

If she had any sense, she would pull out of Rafe's arms, make an excuse and walk away *right now*, but the music seemed to be twining round them, and he was so broad and hard and inviting that in spite of herself Miranda felt herself relaxing instead.

Her mind might be issuing frantic instructions to stiffen every last sinew, but her bones were dissolving with the sheer pleasure of being held. The hand she had laid rigidly against his shoulder softened and of its own volition slid over the immaculate set of his suit, luxuriating in the feel of the powerful muscles beneath as she wondered what it would be like to slide her fingers under his jacket to unbutton his shirt, to spread her hands over his warm, bare skin…

Miranda inhaled sharply, shocked by the vividness with which she could imagine the scene. The sooner this dance ended, the better.

But when the music died away on a last note, perversely she wanted to cry. Rafe stopped moving but he continued to hold her until Miranda tried to tug her hands free.

'They're just getting going,' he said, not letting her go. 'Stay.'

Miranda's throat was tight and hard and it was effort to force the words. 'I think I'd better go,' she managed. 'I've got things to do.'

'Like what?'

Protecting my heart. Remembering who I am and what I'm doing here. Making sure I don't do anything stupid like fall in love with you.

'Just things.' She swallowed. 'I'm sure you'll be able to find another partner for the last dances.'

'I'd rather dance with you,' said Rafe softly, and his voice was deep and warm and irresistible. 'Do you really want to go, Miranda?'

No, Miranda's heart cried, *no, I don't*! But her head was back in control now.

'Yes,' she said, not meeting his eyes.

Rafe let her go at that. 'Then you must go, of course,' he said. 'Thank you for the dance, Miranda,' he said with cool formality. 'And thank you for everything you've done this evening.'

She couldn't let herself look at him properly, or she would simply throw herself back into his arms and beg him not to let her go again, and what kind of behaviour was that for a temporary assistant?

'Goodnight,' she said huskily, and, turning, she hurried away from him, in search of Elvira's shoes, her clipboard and the cold comfort of knowing that she had been sensible.

* * *

Miranda waited for the barman to fill the glasses with champagne before picking up the tray and heading back into the crowd. This was her third night working this week, and she was tired, but she had found herself making excuses not to spend the evenings alone in the flat, where there was too much time to sit and think and remember.

It had been a long three weeks since the ball. She had a new assignment at a management consultancy. Everyone was very nice and if the job was dull, well, temp jobs often were. It was a pity there wasn't more to keep her busy. She had an hour for lunch every day, but there were no walks in the park, no ice creams, no Rafe to tease her and provoke her and make her laugh.

Miranda hadn't realised how much she would miss him.

She had never said a proper goodbye. Back in the office, it had taken a couple of days to tidy her desk and sort out the payment of the outstanding bills, and then she had handed the last few loose ends to Ginny. Rafe hadn't been around.

What had she expected? Miranda asked herself. That he would come rushing back just to say goodbye to a temp? She had done the job she was asked to do, and now that it was over it was time to move on. She'd said goodbye to Ginny and to Simon and promised to keep in touch, but of course she hadn't. It wouldn't be fair to meet up when all she wanted to do was to talk about Rafe, to find out how he was, whether he had missed their walks in the park.

Whether he remembered every second of that dance the way she did.

Enough. Miranda was always having to scold herself for drifting into wistful memories nowadays. Straightening her shoulders and fixing her smile back in place, she moved from group to group, offering champagne. The reception, to launch a new charitable foundation, was being held in a museum, although nobody seemed to be looking at the exhibits. They were all too busy talking. They certainly seemed to be enjoying themselves, Miranda thought, squeezing between guests with her tray held high, and was startled to realise that she was feeling envious.

When was the last time *she* had simply enjoyed herself? Ever since she'd given up her degree course to try—and fail—to sort out the mess at Fairchild's, it seemed that she had been worrying. She had worried about the firm and what would happen to its employees. She had worried about her father, about Octavia, about how they would pay for Belinda's wedding.

She had spent so long worrying about money that she had forgotten *how* to enjoy herself, Miranda realised. Instead, she had fixated on the idea of Whitestones as a place where she could hide away from all the worries associated with London. Everything always seemed so much simpler there.

Well, she would get there, but at her present rate of saving it wasn't going to be any time soon. In the meantime, perhaps it was time to start enjoying the present more, the way Rafe did? Miranda thought about the laughter at the back of his eyes, about the way he exuded energy and a zest for life no matter what he was doing, whether it was just sitting at a desk or eating an ice cream in the park.

The thought of Rafe's smiling eyes was enough to give her a pang, but Miranda caught herself up. Less moping, she ordered herself. Less planning. If she really wanted to change, she would start right now. She would still work, still save, but she would live for now too.

It felt surprisingly good to have made the decision, and Miranda smiled as she offered the last champagnes in exchange for empty glasses. There was just one glass left, she noticed. She might as well go back and get more.

She was turning towards the bar when a voice behind her said, 'I'll take that one,' and she nearly dropped the lot as she spun round, joy blazing through her.

'Rafe!'

There he stood, looking devastatingly handsome in a dinner jacket and bow tie. 'Hello, Miranda,' he said, and smiled.

There ought to be a law against a smile like that. It couldn't be right that a mere curving of the lips, a simple creasing of the cheeks and twinkle of the eyes, could wipe one's brain free of all coherent thought and turn one's bones to liquid. Look at the tray, about to slide from nerveless hands!

Belatedly, Miranda tightened her hold on it and took a grip of herself. 'Hello,' she said. It came out a bit croaky, but it wasn't too bad, considering.

Rafe reached out and helped himself to the glass of champagne. 'How have you been?'

Miserable. Bored. Missing you. 'Oh, fine,' said Miranda. It didn't sound that convincing, so she said it again. 'Fine.'

'I heard you had another job. I trust you've managed to whip the new photocopier into shape?'

'Unfortunately, the assignment ends tomorrow, so I'll have to start training another one next week.'

Yes, that was better. She sounded much more like her old self: cool, composed, in control. 'How are you, anyway?' she asked, keeping her smile steady. 'Are you engaged yet?'

Rafe made a face. 'Nowhere near. I'm not having much success,' he told her. 'I can't find anyone.'

'There must be *somebody*! What happened to all those women we invited to the ball? Haven't you invited any of them out?'

'I have,' said Rafe. 'I asked Julia first. I invited her out to dinner, and pulled out all the stops to make it a romantic evening I thought she would like. It turned out I needn't have bothered.

She told me very kindly that there was no need for me to jump through all the hoops. She said she didn't want an emotional relationship right then and was only interested in sex.'

He smiled crookedly. 'I felt a bit of a fool for going to all that trouble,' he confessed. 'I got the feeling she thought I was a bit weird for wanting something more than her body.'

'Well, now you know what it's like for a lot of women most of the time,' said Miranda, wishing she could ask whether he had slept with Julia anyway.

'Next I invited Stella out. I tried dinner again, but it wasn't any more successful than the last time.'

'Was she only interested in your body too?'

'No, I'd almost have preferred her if she had been. At least Julia was fun. Stella cross-examined me over dinner about everything from my star sign to when I was potty trained.'

'What on earth for?'

'She had a very clear checklist in her head about what she wanted from a man. She's incredibly high-powered and, according to her, she doesn't have the time to waste on getting to know a man who isn't going to tick all the boxes.'

'And you didn't?' said Miranda, surprised.

'Apparently not.'

'So who did you try next?'

'Oh, next it was Isabel. She seemed really nice, and I really thought I was getting somewhere, but when I suggested a second date, she said no. She'd been hurt once before, she said, and she said my track record made her nervous. If I'd got to thirty-five without a serious relationship, she didn't think I would ever be capable of one. So there you are,' he told Miranda. 'Three strikes. At least the restaurants are doing a booming business.'

He spoke lightly, but Miranda had the feeling the charge had hurt him more than he was prepared to admit.

'I obviously haven't been very successful at changing my image,' he went on.

'Perhaps she'd heard about you taking the other two out and thought you were running true to type?'

'You'd think she'd be glad I wasn't divorced and was waiting for the right woman before I made a commitment, but no! You women are never happy!'

'It's a pity you weren't at least engaged before,' Miranda agreed, shifting her tray to the other arm. 'Then she would have known that you had been prepared to commit, but that you'd been hurt. That's a big draw for a lot of women. They love the idea of a man they can rescue.'

'Unfortunately, everyone knows that I was never engaged,' said Rafe. 'Thanks to the gossip magazines they all know more about me than I do!' He paused. 'Unless I could make up an engagement—when I was in Africa, perhaps?'

Miranda's mouth turned down dubiously. 'It would be difficult to carry off. You'd have to make up a whole story and remember it in every detail, and then the press would go off looking for your alleged fiancée…you know what they're like.'

'That's true.' Rafe sighed. 'It wouldn't work unless I could produce the girl and where am I going to find someone prepared to back up a story like that?'

'Well, if you'd like to pay me, I'll do it,' said Miranda flippantly. 'I'm looking for a new job next week!' She looked down at her tray. 'And talking of jobs, I'd better get on with this one.'

She made herself look into his eyes. 'It was good to see you again,' she said, meaning it. For a few moments there, it had been like old times talking together. 'I'm sure you'll find someone soon. Good luck with it!'

Rafe watched her go, straight-backed as ever. He wished she weren't working. He wished he could take her out of here, and go somewhere quiet where they could just talk.

Damn it, he had missed her. He had missed the crispness of her comments, the directness of her gaze, the cool consolation of her presence.

Ever since the ball, he had been feeling edgy. Oh, he had tried. Look at all the women he had invited out! But that was the point: he had to *try* with them. He didn't have to try with Miranda. He could just be himself. She was a friend. Of course he had missed her. It didn't mean he *needed* her. It just meant he wanted to talk to her.

Whenever he went out to a reception or party, Rafe had been hoping to see Miranda among the waitresses, but she was never there, and in the end he had been reduced to looking up the number of the caterers at the ball and calling her friend Rosie to find out when and where she would be working. It hadn't been difficult to get himself invited tonight. He'd just had to make a substantial donation, and all because he had wanted to see a friend!

Rafe was exasperated with himself. Women complained that men like him fought shy of commitment, but he wanted to settle down, he *wanted* to commit. Why was he finding it so hard?

His latest three dates had been salutary experiences. It had been easy taking girls out when he was just amusing himself, but getting them to take him seriously was proving more difficult than he thought.

It had been tempting to blame Miranda. The thought of her was distracting him, and he had hoped that seeing her again would put her in perspective so that he could focus on his search for a suitable bride. That ought to be his priority. God knew, he had spent enough on the ball. He couldn't give up now, just because he had been so happy to see Miranda again.

I'll do it. Her words echoed as he stared morosely down into his untouched glass of champagne. *I need a job.*

She had been joking, of course. Rafe knew that. She didn't mean it.

It would never work, anyway.

Would it?

'You go on home,' said Rosie. 'I've still got things to do.'

'I'll give you a hand,' Miranda offered. 'Then we can go home together.'

But Rosie insisted that she go. There was an air of suppressed excitement about her tonight. Perhaps she had a new man on the go? Shrugging, Miranda picked up her bag and made her way outside. The night air was cool after the heat of the kitchen, and she paused for a moment, breathing it in with relief.

It was only then that she became aware of the sleek car waiting on the double yellow lines outside the entrance, its engine purring and its top down.

Rafe leant over to open the passenger door. 'I'll give you a lift home,' he said.

'It's not exactly on your way,' said Miranda after the first moment of shock.

'I know. Rosie gave me the address.'

'*Rosie* knows you're here?'

'She's trusting me to see you safely home,' said Rafe.

That explained why Rosie had been so keen to see her go.

'I'm perfectly capable of getting the Tube,' Miranda said, but she walked over to the car and got in. Her legs were aching, and she was too tired to make an issue of it. If Rafe wanted to drive around London in the dark, let him.

'I thought you'd gone,' she said unguardedly, and then cursed herself for an idiot. Rafe would think that she had looked for him again. She had, of course, but there was no need for him to know that.

'I've been waiting for you,' said Rafe as he checked the mirror and pulled out into the traffic. 'If you are available and willing, I've got a proposition to put to you.'

She looked at him warily. 'What sort of proposition?'

'Don't worry, it's not the usual one a girl gets when she's picked up from a pavement!' Rafe slanted a smile at her. 'You must be tired after being on your feet all evening. Wouldn't you like to give up waitressing?'

'I can't. It's the only way I can save anything for Whitestones.'

'How much do you think you'll need before you can move down there?'

Miranda sighed. 'Twenty, twenty-five thousand?'

'It'll take a long time to save that on a temp's salary even if you have got an evening job.'

'Thank you for pointing that out,' she said sourly. 'I'd already worked it out for myself!'

'How would you like to earn that in a month?'

Miranda laughed. 'Would I have to do anything illegal?' she asked, thinking that he was joking.

'You might have to lie a bit.'

They had come to a stop at a red light, and she swivelled in her seat to stare at him. 'Are you serious?'

'Completely. I'll pay you twenty-five thousand pounds if you'll pretend to be my fiancée for a month.'

'What?'

'It was your idea,' Rafe pointed out. 'You said you needed a job.'

'I meant a secretarial one!'

'This one would be more fun.'

Fun. Miranda's instinctive refusal died on her lips as the car shot away from the lights. Hadn't she resolved not to take life so seriously? Fun was exactly what was missing in her life at the moment.

If only the thought of spending a month with Rafe would be as simple as fun. Miranda suspected it was more likely to turn her life upside down. It might be shattering or exhilarating or thrilling or dangerously appealing, but simple fun? No, it wouldn't be that.

On the other hand, she could at least listen before she dismissed his proposal out of hand. Still more than half convinced he was joking, she looked at him suspiciously.

'What exactly are you proposing?'

'Just what we talked about. We get engaged, and everyone realises that I'm serious about settling down.'

'But if the engagement doesn't last, you'll just look even more afraid of commitment,' Miranda objected. 'Then you'll be worse off than before.'

'Not if you're the one to dump me,' said Rafe. 'I'm going to be besotted with you for a month, and when you leave I'm going to be broken-hearted. You were the one who said they'd queue up to help me move on and show me what the love of a good woman could do,' he reminded her.

The more he thought about it, the more sense it made. He had examined the strategy from all angles while he was waiting for Miranda to appear, and he could see no obvious flaws in it. It might not work, of course, but it well might, and in the meantime he would get to spend a month with Miranda, which would surely be enough to get her out of his system once and for all.

Miranda, however, was clearly unconvinced. 'Nobody's going to believe that you're besotted with *me*,' she said.

'You underestimate yourself.'

'Perhaps I underestimate your acting ability,' she countered, disgruntled in a way she couldn't begin to explain.

'Then you shouldn't,' said Rafe. 'I bet I could convince everyone I was mad about you.' He glanced at her with a half-smile. 'I really don't think it would be that hard.'

'They'd all think you were odd for choosing someone like me,' said Miranda grouchily.

'No, they wouldn't. They'd think I was perceptive and interesting for being intrigued by a woman who goes out of her way not to draw attention to herself.'

Well, she had asked for it. What had she expected? That he would tell her that she was beautiful and no one would be in the least surprised at his choice?

'That doesn't explain why, having snared myself the most eligible bachelor in Britain, I'd toss him aside after a mere month,' said Miranda after a moment.

Rafe grinned as he turned onto Westminster Bridge. 'Maybe that's what makes you so intriguing?'

She regarded him with exasperation. Didn't he take anything seriously? 'You'd need a better reason than that if people aren't going to realise it's just a big joke!'

'I'm sure we can think of some reason why you don't want to marry me,' said Rafe. 'It has to be one that doesn't make people think I've got some dirty secret, and it can't be because you think I'm having an affair with someone else. Remember, they've got to be sorry for me. You've got to break my heart!'

'Oh, yes, I can see me doing that!'

'Why can't you be the one who's got a problem with commitment?' he suggested, ignoring her sardonic aside. 'Just when I'm ready to settle down, you decide you can't face married life and run off.'

'I'd never be that wet,' said Miranda tartly. 'I'd rather tell everyone that I was bored with you.'

'I'm not paying you twenty-five thousand quid to make me sound dull! That's not the idea at all!'

'Oh, well, if you're going to be picky…' She thought for a moment, getting into the idea in spite of herself. 'I suppose I could say that I don't want children, and that I got cold feet when I realised you were desperate to settle down and start a family.'

'Now, that *is* a good idea,' said Rafe cheerfully. 'They're bound to feel sorry for me when they hear that. Let's agree on that.'

'I haven't agreed to any of it yet,' Miranda reminded him sharply.

'Don't you want to be able to go to Whitestones?'

'You know I do. It's just…well, the whole idea is crazy!'

'Think about it at least,' said Rafe. 'It might be crazy, but it might also be a way to get us both what we want most.'

CHAPTER EIGHT

MIRANDA did think about it as they drove past tower blocks and industrial estates and soulless shopping malls. It was an unattractive part of London, at least that bit of it that could be seen from the main road in the murky orange glow of the street lights. It was all right for Rafe, living in Mayfair with its imposing houses and elegant squares, but Rosie could only afford a tiny flat on the outskirts of London. Miranda hated the journey to and from the city centre where she worked, and longed for Whitestones, where the night was properly dark and the air was clean and where in place of traffic and sirens and jangling alarms all you could hear was the sea on the shingle.

Now she could go.

All she had to do in exchange was pretend to be in love with Rafe for a month.

Why was she even hesitating? Miranda didn't know. She just knew that the thought was enough to flutter the nerves just beneath her skin and make her stomach churn with a disturbing mixture of excitement and fear.

Because, actually, she did know. She was afraid she might enjoy being with Rafe too much. She was afraid she might find it hard to resist him. That she might forget that she was only supposed to be pretending.

But she could do it. She would just have to keep a cool head and keep remembering that it *was* just a pretence. Miranda had a nasty feeling that might be a lot more difficult than it sounded, but wouldn't it be worth it for Whitestones? She would never get a better chance than this to make her dream come true. Was she really going to throw it away because she was afraid of the way Rafe made her feel?

How wet of her *that* would be!

'Well?' Rafe pulled up outside Rosie's flat and switched off the engine. 'I know you've been thinking—could practically hear your mind working!—but have you come to any decision?'

Miranda moistened her lips. 'Twenty-five thousand pounds is a lot of money. What exactly would I have to do for that?'

'Well, let's see…' Rafe undid his seat belt so that he could turn and study her face. 'All we'd have to do is leak our engagement to a couple of gossip columns, and go out together a few times so people can see how in love we are.'

His face was perfectly straight, but there was a familiar undercurrent of laughter in his voice. Miranda hated the way he could do that.

'You'd have to act like a suitably besotted fiancée,' he told her. 'Do you think you could manage that?'

Her chin went up. 'Do I have to be *besotted*?'

'For twenty-five thousand pounds?' Rafe grinned. 'I think besotted is the least you could be, don't you?'

'Well, what do besotted fiancées do?' asked Miranda ungraciously. 'I don't want to spend a month looking adoringly at you! Your ego is quite big enough as it is!'

Rafe's mouth twitched appreciatively. 'Imagine you're in love with me, Miranda. How would you act with me then?'

'Like I do now, probably,' she said, getting out of the car and wishing she could get out of the conversation as easily.

'You don't think you would be a *little* more affectionate if you loved me?' Rafe asked conversationally. 'Everyone has got to think that behind that rather prim and proper exterior is a wild, exciting woman who only I can see. You might have to bring yourself to touch me.' He had followed her to the door of the flat and a smile hovered around his mouth as he looked down at her. 'You know, hold my hand occasionally, even kiss me. Somehow you'd need to give the impression that you can't keep your hands off me.'

Miranda's cheeks felt as if they were on fire. 'Why can't you be the one who can't keep *your* hands off *me*?'

'Oh, I don't see any problem about that,' said Rafe, and smiled in a way that set her heart thudding. 'No, no problem at all...'

Reaching out, he ran a knuckle down the curve of her cheek. It was the gentlest of touches, but it seemed to sear her skin, and Miranda flinched back from it, drawing a sharp, unsteady breath.

Rafe's smile faded. 'But maybe it *is* a problem for you,' he said slowly. 'I can see that you're tense. I don't want to make you uncomfortable. Perhaps we'd better drop the whole idea?'

'No!' Miranda spoke without thinking. Her cheek was still burning where his finger had grazed the skin, and she was mortified at the way she had jerked back from his touch. What was wrong with her? Anyone would think she was a silly schoolgirl, instead of a sensible woman who had just been offered the chance of a lifetime!

She could do this. She could do it for Whitestones. It wasn't as if Rafe were suggesting anything illegal or even immoral. Neither of them were committed to anyone else. They would be acting out a lie, true, but nobody's feelings would be hurt. Rafe wasn't expecting her to sleep with him—at least, she didn't think so. All she had to do was hold his hand occasionally. Of course she could do that.

'No,' she said again. 'It won't be a problem. I'm not a very huggy-kissy person, I suppose, but I can see that if we want to convince everyone that we really are engaged, I'd need to be a bit more demonstrative. I can do that.'

'Really?' Rafe was still looking doubtful.

'Really,' said Miranda.

She was going to have to prove it to him, she realised. She was going to have to kiss him.

Heat washed through her as her eyes rested on his mouth, and a feeling like a fist clenching deep inside her made her inhale slowly. Face it, Miranda, she told herself. Not only can you do it, you *want* to do it.

'Would you like me to prove it?' she asked, and without waiting for an answer she stepped forwards and rested her hands against his chest. Slowly, almost thoughtfully, she spread them so that she could run them up and over his powerful shoulders.

Rafe smiled. 'Why not?' he said softly.

Miranda deliberately didn't hurry. She felt curiously calm. Having got this far, she wasn't going to back down now. If Rafe thought she was going to be content with a hurried peck on the cheek, he was going to discover his mistake. So he thought she was tense, did he? He thought she was prim and proper? Well, this was her chance to show him just how wrong he was.

He was standing very, very still, but there was an arrested expression in his eyes as she savoured the feel of his body beneath her hands. Only the pulse hammering in his cheek gave away his acute awareness of her, and suddenly Miranda was filled with a sense of her own power.

Her mouth curving in a smile of its own, she leant in and pressed her lips to his throat below his ear for a long, breathless moment before she began to tease little kisses along his jaw line. His skin was warm and faintly prickled with stubble, and he smelt comfortingly of clean laundry. Miranda eased herself closer and slid her hands down to slip beneath his jacket. Suddenly it was easy.

With a tiny sigh she reached the corner of his mouth at last. She felt it curve in response, but she kept her exploration soft and seductive, tasting his lips almost reflectively, giving herself up to the sheer bliss of being able to kiss him the way she realised she had wanted to right from the start.

Rafe felt as if he were about to explode. Unable to hold out any longer, he brought his hands up to grip her and yank her closer so that he could deepen the kiss, and Miranda clutched instinctively at his hard, gloriously solid body, anchoring herself against the swirl of sheer pleasure as she struggled to stay in control.

This was *her* kiss. She could kiss him as deeply, as hungrily, as he could kiss her. But her blood was pounding, her whole being pulsing with a joyous excitement that sucked her down in spite of herself as they kissed and kissed and kissed again, spinning her round until she forgot there was a competition, forgot what she was trying to prove, forgot everything except Rafe's mouth and the thrill of his hands hard on her and the *feel* of him.

'Miranda…'

He was kissing her throat, murmuring her name as he fumbled with the buttons of her blouse, and she gasped and tipped back her head, her fingers entwined in his dark hair. Vaguely she became aware of something sharp and solid digging into her back. It was enough to pull her back from the brink, and she flailed for a last shred of control. How had they ended up here? Had Rafe backed her against the door, or had she dragged him with her as she collapsed back onto it for support?

Either way, she had to stop this…*now*, Miranda told herself, even as she shivered and arched beneath the wickedly delicious drift of his lips.

Now, while she still could. Before Rafe peeled her blouse from her shoulders, before she tugged his shirt from his trousers and was unbuckling his belt. Before they stumbled upstairs, shedding clothes as they went, and fell onto her bed together.

From somewhere, Miranda found the strength to disentangle her fingers from his hair and press her palms against his chest to push him away an inch.

'Wait,' she croaked.

Rafe stilled for a moment, and then, very slowly, he levered himself away from her and dropped his hands.

Miranda moistened her lips. She was trembling, and the bones in her legs seemed to have dissolved, leaving only a fizzy sensation to keep her upright.

'I...I think that's made the point,' she said unevenly.

Her lips were swollen, her face flushed, her eyes dark and dazed, and Rafe had to shake his head to clear it.

'I take it all back,' he managed, more shaken than he wanted to admit. He was having trouble with his breathing still. 'There was nothing prim and proper about that kiss.'

'I told you I could do it.'

'You did, and you were right. No one watching you kiss like that would have the slightest difficulty in understanding why I'd want to marry you!'

'I don't think it will be necessary to repeat it,' said Miranda, retreating behind her most prickly manner. 'We'd hardly be likely to kiss in public. At least, not like that.'

'No, perhaps it's better if we don't,' agreed Rafe. 'We're liable to get ourselves arrested if we do!' He smiled down at her. 'I take it, then, that you'll pretend to be my fiancée?'

'It will just be for a month?' Her legs were still very unsteady, but at least her voice sounded like her own again.

'A month,' he confirmed 'At the end of which time, you have to find a way to break off our engagement. In return, I'll give you a cheque for twenty-five thousand pounds. Does that seem fair?'

It was more than fair, Miranda thought.

'I'll do it,' she told him.

'What about this one?'

Rafe picked up a ring with an eye-popping emerald set in a cluster of diamonds, each one of which would have made a spectacular ring on its own. He handed it to Miranda, who slid it reluctantly onto her finger.

It felt awkward and heavy, and looked completely out of place on her hand. Except, of course, it wasn't the ring that was out of place. It was her.

What was she doing here in this exclusive jeweller's, trying on engagement rings? Miranda was beginning to wonder what had possessed her to agree to Rafe's crazy plan. Nobody in their right minds would ever believe that he would seriously consider marrying someone like her!

But Rafe seemed confident. He had immediately started making plans, and insisted on buying her a ring, sweeping aside her objections that it wasn't necessary.

'Of course you have to have a ring,' he had told her. 'You won't look like a fiancée without a socking great diamond on your finger.'

If it had been left to him, they would have been at the jeweller's the very next day, but Miranda had pointed out that it was Friday, and that she had to go to work, even if he didn't.

'They're expecting me. I can't just not turn up.'

'Oh, very well, we'll do it on Saturday then,' Rafe had grumbled. 'When does this assignment end?'

'Tomorrow's my last day.'

'Then you'll be free next week?'

But Miranda had dug in her heels about that, too. Not if the agency can find me a job. I'm not giving up work just to sit around and wait for you to go out in the evenings.'

Rafe regarded her with frustration. 'But you won't need to work,' he said. 'That's why I'm paying you twenty-five thousand pounds!'

'Yes, and how long will that last if I have to live in London on no salary?' Miranda retorted. 'That money is for Whitestones. I'm not wasting it. No, I'm going to keep working until I'm ready to go to Whitestones and not before.'

Rafe had sighed. 'Has anyone ever told you you're a very stubborn woman, Miranda Fairchild? You'd better come back and work at Knighton's, then. Ginny can ring the agency and request you for another temporary assignment.'

'But that's ridiculous!'

'No more ridiculous than the fiancée of one of the richest men in the country insisting on doing some tedious office job,' he pointed out.

'It's not ridiculous to want to work for a living,' said Miranda, exasperated by him. 'Obviously I'd give up working in the evenings,' she told him. 'I'll need to be available to go out so people can see us together.'

'Big of you,' said Rafe, who was feeling oddly disgruntled. 'I was beginning to wonder whether you'd insist on keeping that job, too!'

Infuriatingly, Miranda refused to rise. 'Being seen out with you at social events was part of the deal,' she said coolly. 'Giving up my day job wasn't.'

'I'm hardly going to see you if you're not at Knighton's,' he grumbled. 'Perhaps you'd better move in with me. At least we might spend more than five minutes together then.'

In fact, that was an excellent idea, he decided. He should have thought of that before.

Miranda clearly didn't think it was such a good idea.

'Move in with you? What on earth for?'

'This is the twenty-first century, Miranda. Nobody is going to believe I would marry someone I wasn't sleeping with.'

'Who said anything about sleeping with you?' she demanded, glaring at him. 'That wasn't part of our agreement either!'

Rafe looked at her flushed face, and found himself remembering that kiss with an intensity that took him unawares. He had sensed the warmth and passion simmering beneath her cool surface, but the reality had been so much more exciting than even he had imagined. And if she kissed like that, what would it be like to make love to her?

'Perhaps we should renegotiate,' he suggested, but Miranda wasn't having that.

'Perhaps we should stick to what was agreed,' she said crisply. 'You wanted me to turn up to a few events on your arm and look suitably besotted, and that's *all* I agreed to!'

'You agreed that you would do your best to convince people that we were really engaged. What kind of engagement are they going to think we have if it gets out that I'm driving you chastely home every night?'

Rafe dragged a hand through his hair. Why was nothing ever easy with Miranda?

'Look, you can have your own room,' he offered. 'I'm not suggesting that we spend every night making mad, passionate love!'

He had thought about it, though, hadn't he? He pushed the thought aside.

'It's not as if I'm short of space,' he went on, thinking about the house he had inherited along with the company from his father. 'My housekeeper is very discreet. Nobody else need know that we're not actually sleeping together.'

Miranda hesitated. The thought of living with Rafe was enough to set her prickling with nerves, but, having got her way about working, it was her turn to compromise. Besides, it made a kind of sense.

'All right,' she said. 'I'll move in—on condition that I have my own room.'

'Since we're talking about conditions…' said Rafe, surprised at how triumphant he felt at having convinced Miranda to come and live with him. It wasn't even as if they were going to be sleeping together! He must be losing his touch.

She looked at him suspiciously. 'What?'

'You need to do something about your clothes. Octavia can take you shopping after we've bought a ring.'

'What's wrong with my clothes?' Miranda bristled immediately.

'We're going to be going out in the evenings a lot and you can't wear those awful suits you insist on,' he told her. '*Or* your waitressing outfit, come to that,' he said before she could suggest it. 'Unless you'd like to wear that cat suit again?' The dark eyes gleamed with the memory of how revealingly it had clung to her figure. 'That would get you noticed!'

Faint colour tinged Miranda's cheekbones. 'I couldn't possibly wear that again,' she said. 'The tail was *so* last season!'

Mentally, she reviewed her limited wardrobe. She had never been much of one for clothes, even before Fairchild's had collapsed. Belinda and Octavia had always been obsessed with fashion, but Miranda had stubbornly resisted all their attempts to smarten her up. She wore suits for work, and the rest of the time she was happy in jeans and a T-shirt. They were fine for going to a film, or having a drink with Rosie, but she might have to make more of an effort for the kind of occasions Rafe clearly had in mind.

'I suppose I could get something for the evenings,' she said grudgingly, 'but I don't need Octavia. Her taste is quite different from mine.'

Rafe looked at her with amusement. 'You have lots of wonderful qualities, Miranda, but style is not one of them,' he told her frankly. 'Your sister, on the other hand, has it in spades.'

'Why not pretend to be engaged to *her*, then?' Miranda asked snippily. 'Why bother with me if I'm such a mess?'

'I prefer you,' said Rafe.

There was a tiny pause. *I prefer you.* Hardly the most romantic declaration, but Miranda felt suddenly hot as her eyes met his, and the silence seemed to sizzle around the edges.

With an effort, she wrenched her gaze away. 'Why can't you prefer me as I am, then? Why do I have to be tricked out like everyone else?' She felt scratchy and cross. 'I can't stand all that prinking and preening,' she grumbled. 'I hate pretending to be something I'm not.'

'But that's what you do every time you put on one of those dark uniforms of yours,' said Rafe, gesturing at what she was wearing and barely able to contain his frustration. '*That's* pretending. It's pretending you're not warm and intelligent and attractive and interesting and *sexy*. It's pretending you're just a dowdy mouse, terrified someone is going to notice you and make you *live* a little!'

At the time Miranda had stared at him in stunned silence for a moment before blustering that he was talking rubbish, but now as she looked down at the emerald sparkling on her finger she thought again about what he had said. She had nice hands. They were slim, with slender fingers and nails that were short but well shaped and very clean, but she had never drawn attention to them with jewellery or polish, just as she never drew attention to herself with stylish clothes or make-up.

Was Rafe right? *Was* she afraid to seize life with both hands? She had always been so used to her sisters and parents grabbing the attention that she had grown accustomed to not being noticed. Miranda had told herself that she didn't need the limelight the way they did, but could the truth have been that she was scared to compete with them because she knew she would fail?

Miranda didn't like to think of herself like that. She wanted to believe that she was cool and capable, not terrified, not scared, not afraid.

She *wasn't* afraid, of *anything*, and she would prove it, to Rafe and to herself. Instinctively, she squared her shoulders. This pretend engagement had made her stupidly jittery, but that was silly. It was a straightforward arrangement. Rafe hadn't forced her into it. She had made the choice on her own, and now it was up to her to make a success of it.

She would keep her side of the bargain, Miranda vowed. She would be a fiancée Rafe could be proud of, and when she left everyone would understand why he was sorry to see her go. Nobody would even suspect that it had all been planned.

Slowly, she drew the ring off her finger. 'It's beautiful, but I don't think it's really me,' she said. She put it down on the velvet tray and pointed to a dazzling band of square-cut diamonds.

'May I try that one?'

Rafe picked it up and took her left hand so that he could slide it onto her finger. 'It fits perfectly, Cinderella,' he said and, although he was smiling, there was an expression in his eyes that made Miranda's heart trip.

'So it does,' she said breathlessly.

'Does that make me Prince Charming?' asked Rafe.

He was acting, too, Miranda reminded herself. Firmly, she brought her breathing back under control. 'I think it must do!' she said with what she hoped was a flirtatious look.

'A very stylish choice,' the jeweller approved.

Miranda turned her hand this way and that to admire the dazzle of the diamonds and then smiled at Rafe, the personification of a besotted fiancée. 'May I have this one, darling?' At least she didn't need to worry about whether he could afford it or not. He could have bought the whole shop without so much as a dent in his bank account.

'You can have whatever you want,' he told her, his voice deep and warm and his smile appreciative of the effort she was making.

The diamonds flashed in the light as Miranda laid her hand against his cheek. 'Thank you,' she said softly.

With one part of her mind she was aware that this was the kind of thing a girl would do when her fiancé had bought her a beautiful ring, but the other part wasn't thinking at all. It was just that he was there, smiling at her, and her hand had lifted of its own accord.

He was freshly shaved and his skin was smooth and warm beneath her fingers. If she had been thinking, she would have left it as a brief caress, but it felt so good to touch him that Miranda's hand lingered. Still smiling, Rafe turned his head, lifting his own hand at the same time to capture hers so that he could press a kiss against her palm.

It was a very gentle kiss, with none of the wild excitement they had shared at the door to Rosie's flat, but Miranda felt it right down to her toes. His lips were warm and sure and infinitely exciting, and when he parted them to touch the tip of his tongue to her skin an erotic shock jolted through her.

Heat flooded through her, swamping her with a dizzying rush of desire and driving everything else from her head. She forgot the jeweller, watching benevolently. She forgot the role she was supposed to be playing. She forgot everything, in fact, except Rafe, Rafe with his blue, smiling eyes and his warm, smiling mouth and his lean, masculine, irresistible body.

Miranda wanted to climb onto his lap, and pull her hand away from his lips so that she could press her mouth to his, and kiss him properly. She wanted to taste that wickedly delicious tongue and twine her own around it. And that wouldn't be enough, either. She wanted to pull off that immaculately knotted tie and unbutton his pristine shirt and drag it off him. She wanted to fall with him off the ridiculously spindly chair and make love right there on the expensive carpet.

The yearning was so strong that the breath snarled in Miranda's throat, and her heart pounded. She was terrified by how clearly she could imagine it, how much she wanted it. By how close she had come to losing control and simply launching herself at him.

Terrified? There was that word again.

Miranda caught herself up just in time. She wasn't terrified of anything, remember?

A little shakily, she drew her hand away. See, she was perfectly in control. Tilting her chin, she gave Rafe a brilliant smile.

In spite of her bravado, Miranda still felt boneless and unsteady when they left the jeweller's. Rafe opened the door for her, and his hand at the small of her back seemed to burn through her shirt.

'Where are you meeting Octavia?'

'Harvey Nichols.'

'I'll get you a taxi.'

Rafe had barely lifted a hand before a black cab on the other side of the road turned right across four lanes of traffic to pull smartly up to the kerb in front of them.

Miranda eyed him with something close to resentment, although truth to tell she was also relieved to find that irritation had dissipated at least some of that agonising awareness. It was much easier to remember that this was all just a pretence when Rafe was making arrogant assumptions about what she wanted.

'What if I'd wanted to take the bus?'

But Rafe only grinned at her expression. 'Now, don't spoil it, Miranda,' he said, opening the door with a flourish. 'Or should I call you darling? You've been doing a wonderful impression of a besotted fiancée so far!'

Miranda's gaze slid away from his. Only minutes ago she had been fantasising about ripping his clothes off and making love on the carpet, she remembered uncomfortably. What if Rafe had been able to read the naked desire in her eyes? She cringed at the thought. As if he didn't find her amusing enough as it was!

She lifted her chin and bared her teeth at him as she got into the taxi. 'Just doing what I'm being paid for, *darling*.'

'If you carry on like that for a month, you'll be worth every penny of that twenty-five grand!' said Rafe. He handed the driver a note through the window and told him to take Miranda to Knightsbridge.

'I'll meet you later,' he said, preparing to close the door on her. 'I'm putting you in Octavia's hands, remember. I've given her a credit card, so you're to let her use it,' he added with mock sternness. 'I want to see you transformed!' And before Miranda had a chance to object, he had shut the door and banged on the roof of the taxi to tell the cabbie to drive on.

Rather to Miranda's surprise, Octavia was waiting for her as promised. Naturally, she spotted the ring right away.

'Ooh, that is *fabulous*! You lucky, lucky thing, Miranda!'

Miranda had been a little nervous about how Octavia would react to news of the engagement. Expecting scornful disbelief that she had apparently captured someone like Rafe, she had been astounded when Octavia had barely blinked.

'I *thought* something might be up at the ball,' she had said.

'You *did*?' Miranda goggled at her, unable to hide her amazement. 'I mean…even I didn't know then.'

'It was just something about the way you and Rafe were dancing together,' said Octavia carelessly. 'Not that my nose isn't severely out of joint,' she went on, wagging a perfectly manicured finger at Miranda and pretending to sound cross. 'Now I'm going to have to find myself another billionaire!'

She had taken it so well, in fact, that Miranda felt guilty

about not telling her the truth, but they had agreed that not even Rafe's grandmother would know that the engagement wasn't a real one. As Rafe pointed out, if it came out that they had been fooling everyone, he could wave goodbye to any chance of ever being taken seriously.

'What we need is to make sure everyone knows about our engagement without looking as if we want any publicity,' he said. He had proposed leaking the news to a journalist, but Miranda had pooh-poohed that idea.

'I'll just tell Belinda and Octavia, and swear them to secrecy,' she said. 'It'll be all over town in no time at all.'

Sure enough, a snippet had already appeared in the gossip column of an evening paper, and an extraordinary number of school friends Miranda hadn't heard from for years had rung her up to congratulate her enviously and angle for invitations to the wedding.

Belinda was beside herself with excitement and was already pestering Miranda to set a date and pick a designer for her dress. Octavia had been rather more restrained, though her eyes had lit up when Rafe had handed her a credit card and charged her to transform Miranda's wardrobe.

'And you're not to let Miranda take charge of this,' he instructed her. 'She'll just choose the cheapest thing there is and give what's left to a dogs' home!'

Now Miranda hugged her sister and let her admire the ring, but she was conscious that Octavia had been preoccupied recently, and that, although she was as lovely as ever, she wasn't her usual frivolous self. She hadn't been paying her little sister enough attention, Miranda thought guiltily. It would be good to spend a day together and find out what was going on.

'Is everything OK, Tavvy?' she asked as they stepped onto the escalator. 'You look tired.'

'Oh, yes, I'm fine,' said Octavia with a fair assumption of

her usual nonchalance. 'It's just such a bore having to get up for work every morning! This working business certainly cuts into partying time, doesn't it?'

To Miranda's delight, Octavia had suddenly announced after the ball that she had got herself a job. 'It's only temporary,' she warned when Miranda congratulated her. 'I'm only doing it to show Simon I'm not completely useless! He told me I wouldn't last a week.'

Simon, it appeared, knew just how to handle Octavia. Miranda was hopeful that her sister would come to realise what a kind, decent man he was, but even she had to admit that the quiet, steady Simon was an unlikely match for her frivolous little sister.

'How is Simon?' she asked now.

'How would I know? I never see him.' Octavia tossed her hair back and lifted her chin. 'Not that I'd want to, of course! It's not as if he's any fun.'

'Right,' said Miranda. She was tempted to smile at the way Octavia kept insisting that she wasn't attracted to Simon, even though the truth was glaringly obvious to everyone else, but then she remembered how steadfastly she had refused to admit just how attractive Rafe was. She was in no position to mock Octavia for protesting too much, after all!

'Anyway, enough about boring old Simon,' said Octavia with forced gaiety. She waved the credit card Rafe had given her in front of Miranda's face. 'We've got shopping to do!'

CHAPTER NINE

BY THE time they met Rafe for a glass of champagne as agreed, Miranda was exhausted and her feet were aching. Shopping was much harder work than being a waitress, she had decided. Octavia had bullied her in and out of a seemingly endless series of outfits, and then made her spend hours choosing the perfect accessories until they were both laden with carrier bags.

All she wanted now was to sit down, but Octavia made her change before Rafe saw her. 'Put on the pale blue dress,' she ordered, propelling her across the hotel lobby towards the Ladies. 'And don't forget the shoes!'

Too tired to argue, Miranda did as she was told, and even she had to admit that it was a lovely dress when it was on. A vibrant cobalt-blue, it was little more than a sleeveless shift that relied on the fabric and the beautiful cut for its effect. From the front it was very simple, but the back had a stunning strap detail that left a lot of her back bare. It meant she couldn't wear a bra with it, and the silk lining slithered seductively against her skin, making her feel as if she were naked somehow.

Making her feel sexy.

Miranda shivered slightly, and the silk slithered some more.

Slipping on slingbacks with kitten heels, she concentrated fiercely on brushing out her hair. 'And leave it loose!' Octavia ordered. She inspected Miranda critically when she had finished, and then, apparently satisfied, handed her a lipstick.

'Don't even *think* about arguing,' she warned.

'For heaven's sake!' Miranda rolled her eyes, but leant obediently towards the mirror to outline her mouth carefully. '*Now* can I have a glass of champagne?'

'You can.' Octavia linked an arm through hers. 'I can't wait to see Rafe's face.'

Rafe was waiting for them in the bar. He had been keeping an eye on the door, and he got to his feet, smiling, when they appeared at last.

Then he stopped dead, and stood staring. Was that *Miranda*? The only thing he recognised about her was that very straight back as she walked towards him. She was looking slender and very chic in a little blue dress that stopped above the knee and revealed those spectacular legs, and her hair swung shining to her shoulders. She had been stunningly elegant at the ball, but today she looked younger, brighter, *sexier*.

Rafe's mouth dried.

He didn't even notice Octavia until she prodded him out of his stupor. 'Well?' she demanded. 'What do you think?

Think? How could he be expected to *think*?

Rafe couldn't take his eyes off Miranda. 'You look…you look…'

Unable to find the words for how she looked, he simply gave up and reached for her instead. Taking her by the waist, he pulled her towards him and kissed her full on the mouth. Her hands full of carrier bags, she swayed into him, and her lips parted on a tiny gasp, and she tasted so sweet and so *right* that his head reeled.

Without thinking, his hands slid down over her hips and curved around her bottom to pull her closer. The carrier bags dropped unnoticed from Miranda's hands and she lifted them against his chest, curling her fingers into his shirt as she melted into him with a soft, inarticulate murmur deep in her throat.

If it hadn't been for Octavia loudly and pointedly clearing her throat, Rafe would have lost control then, but as it was he retained just enough sanity to remember that he was kissing Miranda in the middle of a busy bar and that unzipping the blue dress and peeling it off her right there and then was probably not an option.

Reluctantly, he lifted his head and let Miranda go.

'Well,' said Octavia, grinning, 'that lipstick was a waste of time, wasn't it? She looks gorgeous, though, doesn't she?'

'I couldn't have put it better myself,' said Rafe, but his voice sounded very odd, as if it came from someone else altogether, and he was excruciatingly aware of Miranda beside him, her face flaming, and carrier bags scattered at her feet. She was trembling slightly, and Rafe didn't blame her. He needed to sit down himself.

Octavia laughed. 'I think you just did!' she said, and deposited the last of her own bags around a chair before she plopped herself down into it. 'Now, where's that champagne you promised?'

What had he done? Rafe asked himself that several times a day over the next two weeks. On one level he was able to function quite normally. He smiled, he talked, he made conversation. He went to work and ran business meetings and even managed a tricky but ultimately successful negotiation.

But inside he was in turmoil. He had asked Octavia to transform her, and that was what she had done, with spectacular success. Rafe was intensely proud of Miranda. He knew she was uncomfortable with the idea of dressing up, but she was sticking to her part of the bargain. Every day, she wore one of the outfits that Octavia had insisted that she buy, and she looked wonderful in them all. It was like seeing a butterfly struggling out of a chrysalis. Couldn't she *see* what the clothes did for her?

Everyone else certainly could, and that was the trouble, Rafe admitted to himself. If he was honest, he wished now that he had never sent her off with Octavia and that credit card. There was a shameful part of him that wished Miranda had stayed just as she was, brisk and practical, dowdy and prim. He had had her to himself then.

Now it was like the ball all over again, but every day. Wherever they went, she was noticed. The women looked at her clothes, and the men looked at her figure with hot eyes that made Rafe clench his jaw.

This was what he had wanted, he reminded himself endlessly. He had wanted Miranda to look like the kind of woman he would marry, but she was just supposed to look attractive and serious and suitable. She wasn't supposed to look *beautiful*. She wasn't supposed to be desirable. It was incredible to think that she had once passed unnoticed through a party with a tray of canapés. Now everybody noticed her.

But nobody noticed her as much as he did. It was torture living in the same house, trying to sleep at night knowing that she was in bed across the landing, soft sheets against her skin, silky hair tumbled over her face.

That was his fault too, Rafe knew. He had insisted that Miranda moved in. He had insisted on all of it.

He was a fool.

He couldn't even blame any of it on Miranda, who was behaving perfectly, and that just made it worse. Why couldn't she go back to being difficult? Instead, she went quietly off to work every day in one of her old suits, as cool and crisp and capable as ever. When she came back at night, she would change into one of the outfits Octavia had chosen so cleverly, and together they would go out, to drinks, to a reception, to dinner, to a party, so that, having missed her all day, he had to share her with everyone else at night.

She never complained, although Rafe knew that she must be bored and dreaming of Whitestones. She was keeping to her part of the bargain absolutely. No one watching her would ever guess that she wasn't wildly in love with him, and there was no doubt that people were starting to look at him differently too, now they could see that he had settled down and chosen to marry someone so obviously not just a party girl.

He ought to be pleased, Rafe knew that too. He ought to be *delighted*, but the truth was that he didn't like the fact that Miranda was just acting when she took hold of his arm, or leant against his shoulder, or smiled as she twined her fingers round his. She showed off her ring with just the right amount of bashful pride, as if she couldn't quite believe her luck.

How was he supposed to concentrate on meeting a suitable bride when she was touching him like that, looking like that?

Pretending like that.

Because, of course, that was all she was doing. Pretending.

Ridiculously, he found himself making excuses to go home early so that he could spend some time with her before they went out. One day, she was just going up the steps to the front door when he met her. It was still warm, and she was wearing a plain short-sleeved blouse with a neat grey skirt and serviceable shoes, and still his throat closed with desire.

'You're late back today,' he said.

'They asked me if I would stay on and finish something for a big meeting tomorrow.'

Rafe could feel a muscle in his jaw beginning to twitch. It was childish, and he despised himself for it, but he hated the fact that Miranda spent her day with strangers, and was prepared to put in extra effort for them, exactly as she had done for him. He hated not being able to think of a single good reason why she shouldn't.

'You look tired,' he said roughly. 'Why don't we just stay in tonight?'

Her eyes flickered. 'But it's the reception at the human rights centre.'

'We don't have to go,' said Rafe as he unlocked the door. 'We can stay in, get a takeaway, watch television…be normal.'

'I'm not here to be normal,' she said, looking at him with those clear eyes that seemed to see right through him. 'I'm here to change your image, so that you can meet the kind of woman you really want to marry.'

The kind of women she insisted on finding wherever they went. She made a point of introducing them to him, and then leaving to talk to someone else, like a cat depositing a mouse at his feet.

Rafe hated that, too.

'And to earn twenty-five thousand pounds,' he said savagely. 'Let's not forget that!'

'I don't,' said Miranda, infuriatingly composed. 'Why do you think I get dressed up every night?'

It wasn't for him.

'There will be lots of interesting women there tonight,' she went on after a moment. 'I think we should go.'

Clearly she didn't want to stay in with him, anyway. Rafe scowled as he held the door open for her. 'It's up to you.'

'Don't *you* want to go?'

How could he tell her now that he didn't? That he wanted to stay here with her, to lie on the sofa with his head on her lap and tell her about his day? To listen to her crisp comments about the people she worked with, and make her laugh? To breathe in the fresh, clean fragrance of her and forget everything else?

He couldn't tell her that she was the only woman he could think about. Miranda didn't want him. She wanted Whitestones and a dog and the sea.

And he didn't want her either, Rafe told himself. At least, he added fairly, he didn't *want* to want her. What was the point of wanting someone determined to run away and live alone by the sea? He needed someone to share his life in London, to support him in making Knighton's his own. He couldn't do that in a tumbledown cottage that didn't even have a phone line.

Rafe could see the door to his father's old study as he followed Miranda into the hall. He remembered his father sitting behind his desk and glowering at him.

'The trouble with you, boy, is that you never stick at anything,' he would despair.

His father had been right, Rafe realised.

Well, now he had changed. He was going to prove his father wrong. He had got over infatuations before, and he would get over Miranda. Maybe tonight was the night he would meet a gorgeous, intelligent, funny woman who would marry him and have his children and be there for him long after Miranda had gone.

No, he had made a plan, and he would stick with it. He had made a deal with Miranda, and he would stick with that, too.

'Of course I want to go,' he said.

Miranda opened the wardrobe and contemplated the array of dresses without enthusiasm. Her heart had leapt when Rafe had suggested that they stay at home, but she hadn't dared accept. She didn't trust herself.

Funny, she had always thought those weeks when Fairchild's finally collapsed would be the most difficult she ever had to face, but in some ways the last fortnight had been harder. Miranda had given up trying to convince herself that she wasn't in love with Rafe, but the more she agonised over it, the more hopeless it seemed. Rafe had made it very clear what he wanted. He didn't believe in the fairy tale. He wasn't going to fall in love, and, even if he did, it wouldn't be with someone like her, now would it?

Get real, Miranda would tell herself dolefully. She could dress up in a few fancy dresses, but they didn't change the person she was underneath. She was still plain Miranda Fairchild, and she still hankered for the tranquillity of Whitestones, where she had felt loved and accepted for herself.

Where she had been happy.

Where she longed to be happy again.

There was no point in dreaming that Rafe would give up his billion-dollar inheritance for a tumbledown cottage by the sea. He had things to prove to himself, and to the father who had died before he could appreciate the man his son had become. Besides, there were lots of women out there who would be happy to stay in London and make him the perfect wife. Miranda knew only too well that she wasn't what Rafe needed, and that if she let herself imagine for one minute that she was, she would only get hurt.

She didn't want to be hurt. She wanted to be happy, and she *would* be once she got to Whitestones.

In the meantime, Miranda could only protect her heart the best she could, but it was agony being with Rafe, but not really being with him, touching him but not really touching him, kissing him, but not the way she wanted to.

Not the way they had kissed outside Rosie's flat. Not the way she had fantasised about kissing him at the jeweller's. The taste of his mouth and the feel of his lean, hard body was lodged in her brain, in the very fibre of her, in every cell beneath her skin, where the memory simmered constantly, flaring the instant Rafe walked into the room or took her hand or smiled.

Which he did a lot. They were supposed to be engaged, after all, and Rafe was doing a very good impression of being in love with her. Look at the way he had kissed her in that bar, as if she were the only person in the world for him. Miranda's heart cracked whenever she remembered the piercing sweetness of that kiss. It had felt so *real*.

But, of course, it hadn't been real. Rafe kept his kisses for public display only. He never touched her when they were alone. He barely smiled at her. Ever since they had embarked on this pretence, in fact, he had been distant, and even brusque at times, and Miranda missed the easy friendship they had once had. Perhaps Rafe, too, was regretting that they had ever started this, but it was too late to go back now. It was only for another couple of weeks, after all, and then she would be gone.

Squaring her shoulders, Miranda pulled a red dress that she hadn't worn before from the wardrobe, and went into the bathroom to put on her make-up. It was surprising how quickly she had got used to getting ready every night.

Would she get used to missing Rafe as quickly?

He was waiting for her at the foot of the grand staircase, looking immaculate as ever in one of his designer suits and a pale blue shirt and tie. His hair was still damp from the shower, and he smelled clean and expensive. For an unguarded moment, Miranda let herself imagine what it might have been like if they had showered together, but jerked her mind away from the tantalising fantasy just in time, and put on a bright smile instead.

'Sorry, have you been waiting long?'

Something had flared in Rafe's eyes as she came down the staircase, but by the time she reached the bottom they were shuttered once more.

'Not at all,' he said, as carefully polite as Miranda.

'I had a call from my grandmother today,' he said as they went out to find a taxi. 'She's invited us down to spend the night this weekend. I couldn't think of a way to refuse. I feel bad enough about deceiving her as it is. She was so delighted to hear about our supposed engagement.'

'Do you think we should tell her the truth?'

Rafe made a face. 'Then her housekeeper would know, and the gardener, and God knows who else. I lose track of everyone who works there. I'm not entirely sure I'd trust Elvira to keep it to herself either,' he said. 'She's not above a good gossip. I think we'd better leave things as they are,' he decided, looking up and down the street for a cab. 'She might be disappointed, but she'll get over it.'

'I'd like to see Elvira again,' Miranda said. It was another hot, clammy evening and she lifted the hair from the back of her neck in a vain attempt to cool it. She wouldn't have this problem if Rafe and Octavia would let her tie her hair up. 'It'll be lovely to get out of the city, too,' she added with a sigh. 'It's been so muggy recently. Sometimes I feel as if I can't breathe.'

'You'll be at Whitestones soon,' Rafe reminded her as he hailed a black cab that had just turned into the square.

'Yes,' Miranda agreed, but to her horror she realised she sounded a bit mournful. Quickly she pinned on a bright smile. 'I can't wait!'

In the meantime, there was at least the prospect of a weekend in the country to look forward to, and Miranda was ready bright and early on Saturday morning, feeling more cheerful than she had for some time.

Rafe was driving his Ferrari, just as he had the first time they had driven down to Knighton Park. He tossed Miranda's overnight bag in the boot, slammed it shut and got in beside her.

'Ready?'

'Absolutely,' she said. 'I'm looking forward to getting away from it all, even if it is just for a night.'

The words were barely out of her mouth before her phone beeped to say that she had a text message. The trouble with mobile phones was that you never could entirely get away from it all. Miranda rummaged in her bag as Rafe waited for a bus to pass so that he could turn out of the quietness of the leafy square.

'It's Octavia.' Miranda read the text and sighed. 'Oh, dear.'

'What's up?'

'She's in love, but she's not finding it easy. I had a coffee with her yesterday, and she was in a bad way. Octavia's used to men being in love with her, but it's not usually the other way round. She says she's never felt like this before.'

'Who's she in love with?' asked Rafe, easing into the traffic.

'Simon.'

'My Simon?'

'Well, I'm not sure that's how he'd choose to describe himself, but, yes, Simon your communications director.'

Rafe whistled soundlessly. 'He doesn't seem like the kind of guy to appeal to Octavia.'

'I know, it's odd, isn't it?' said Miranda. 'He's always seemed to disapprove of Octavia. Maybe there's something in opposites attracting after all.'

'And what does Simon think about Octavia?'

'Well, that's the question. Octavia doesn't know. She's afraid that he thinks she's silly and superficial, but there must be more to it than that. They went to the ball together, if you remember.'

'I didn't notice them,' said Rafe with a sidelong glance and a slight emphasis on the last word, and the air between them thrummed suddenly with the memory of the dance they had shared. Miranda could still feel the solidity of his body, the strength of his hands, the tantalising nearness of his throat.

Swallowing, she made herself look away. 'I think they'd be good together,' she said, determinedly cheerful. 'Simon has got the steadiness that Octavia needs, and she'd give him the fun that's missing in his life.'

Rafe raised his brows. 'Do you really think Simon is Octavia's happy ever after?'

'Perhaps,' said Miranda. 'But of course *you* don't,' she went on with just a trace of bitterness 'You don't believe in fairy tales, do you?'

'I just think you should be careful about letting love—or

lust—blind you to reality. Simon's quite a bit older than Octavia. What if she gets bored? What if he realises he'd have been better off with a sensible wife his own age?'

'What if they *don't*?' she retorted, pressing the reply button on her phone. 'What if they've found the one person who can make them feel complete? What if they're not going to waste time thinking about all the reasons it might not work, but think about spending the rest of their lives being happy instead?'

Rafe shot her a sidelong look as she began texting. 'So what are you saying to Octavia?'

'I think she should tell Simon how she feels.'

'Bit of a risk, don't you think?'

'Sometimes you have to take a risk to get what you really want,' said Miranda.

'Sometimes the hard thing is knowing what it *is* you really want,' said Rafe.

'I know what I want,' she said.

She wanted to be happy. Was that too much to ask? She wanted to be at Whitestones, with someone who would love her just the way she was, not dressed up like a doll every evening. She wanted a man who was utterly necessary to her, and for whom she was utterly necessary in her turn, who wanted to spend his life with her because the thought of not being with her would leave him feeling always incomplete.

Not a man who thought marriage was about practicalities, who could draw up a list of qualities he wanted in a bride and calmly set out to do whatever it took to find her, as if he were picking her out of a catalogue. Not a man whose dancing eyes and seductive smile made it all too easy to forget that his mind was coolly focused on what he wanted, which was absolutely not to live in a derelict cottage with a plain, bossy temp.

It was just as well she had remembered that.

Rafe glanced at her averted profile. 'Ah, yes,' he returned. 'You want the fairy tale.'

There was a note in his voice that Miranda couldn't quite identify, but which she suspected was mockery, and her chin came up. 'Exactly,' she said. 'Nothing else will do.'

It had been a warm but overcast day when they set off, but the sky cleared as they drove west and by the time they reached Knighton Park the sun was shining. Elvira opened the door herself, and the dogs rushed out to meet them, barking and squirming with excitement.

Laughing, Miranda bent to greet them as they jumped up, desperate to lick her, or rolled over, begging her to pat their stomachs, tails wagging furiously.

Lucky dogs.

Rafe felt something unlock around his heart as he watched her crouch down to fuss over the dogs. The cool, sophisticated beauty who had been masquerading so effectively as his fiancée was gone, and she was Miranda again. He hadn't realised until then how much he had missed her.

Elvira was beaming from the steps. Feeling bad about deceiving her, Rafe swept her up in a hug.

'So, at last you've done something sensible,' she said.

She kissed Miranda, who came up escorted by a swarm of over-excited dogs. 'Come in, come in,' she said, leading the way into the vast hall. 'Lunch is nearly ready.'

She had put the two of them in the same room, she explained as she led the way along to her sitting room. 'I know what you're all like,' she said, oblivious to the look Miranda exchanged with Rafe, 'so there's no need for you to creep up and down the corridors, Rafe. I wasn't born yesterday.'

There was a tiny silence. 'I'm shocked, Elvira,' Rafe pretended to joke, playing for time. 'Whenever I've brought girlfriends down in the past, you've always insisted on me sleeping in a separate wing!'

'You weren't engaged before,' she told him, as if that changed everything.

Miranda took the dogs for a long walk after lunch while Elvira strolled slowly around the walled garden on her grandson's arm. Later, she played Scrabble with Miranda, and then Rafe was there to keep her company while Miranda took her time having a shower and changing for the evening.

So it wasn't until Elvira proudly showed them to their room later that night that Miranda and Rafe were alone together. 'I've had a lovely evening,' she said, kissing them both. 'You've made me very happy.'

There was utter silence in the room as Rafe closed the door behind them, and they listened to Elvira shuffling off down the corridor.

'I'm sorry about this,' said Rafe at last. 'I never thought for a minute she'd put us in the same room. She's always been so strait-laced before.'

'It's fine,' said Miranda, wandering over to the big bay window and trying not to look at the vast bed. 'There was no point in making a fuss.'

'I can find somewhere else to sleep tonight,' he offered. 'She'll never know.'

'No.' Miranda drew a deep breath and turned from the window to face him across the room. She had had time to think this afternoon while she was walking the dogs. 'There's no need for that,' she said, surprised to find that her voice was quite steady. 'I was wondering if we should renegotiate the terms of our deal for tonight.'

Rafe was still standing with his back to the door, but his eyes were dark and alert. 'Which particular clause were you thinking of?'

Miranda moistened her lips. 'The one where we don't sleep together.'

'What are you proposing instead?'

'That we do.'

This time the silence stretched until it strummed. Rafe didn't move until, abruptly, he levered himself away from the door and crossed the room. He stopped a few feet from where Miranda stood, straight backed and chin up, in the window.

'You want to sleep with me?'

'Just for tonight,' she said quickly.

Still he didn't move. 'You don't have to do this, Miranda,' he said. 'Do you know how many bedrooms there are in this place? I can easily find somewhere to kip.'

'I want to do it.' Miranda ran the tip of her tongue over her lips again. 'I've been thinking about it all day. I was remembering how I told Octavia she would need to take a risk for what she wanted, and I realised I never do that. I never have.'

Swallowing, she made herself look straight into his eyes. 'You once told me that I was scared, and I think that might be true. I *am* scared. I'm afraid of losing control. When I was growing up, the rest of my family seemed to thrive on chaos, but I hated it. I learnt to be sensible and steady, because that way I felt safe, but I never got what I wanted either.'

'And what do you want now, Miranda?' Rafe's voice was very deep and it seemed to reverberate across the floor and up Miranda's spine.

'I want one night where I don't have to be sensible,' she said without taking her eyes from his. 'I want to not think about the future or the pretence or…or about anything. I want to be able to touch you and feel you and…'

She trailed off, unnerved by his silence. What was she *doing*, asking Rafe Knighton to make love to her, Rafe who must have made love to countless women far more beautiful and desirable than she? It was nice of him not to laugh in her face.

'But only if you want to, of course,' she finished lamely.

Rafe smiled then. Closing the gap between them, he cupped her face very lightly between his hands, feathering his thumbs over her cheekbones, along her jaw, tracing the line of her mouth.

'I think I might force myself,' he teased, but his blue eyes were serious and intent.

She bit her lip. 'Are you sure?'

'Are *you*?'

'Yes, I'm sure.'

And she was. She had gone too far to turn back now and, anyway, he was there, touching her, smiling. Miranda knew that she might—almost certainly *would*—regret it later, but for now this was all she wanted, and it felt completely right.

'In that case,' said Rafe, 'I can tell you that this is all I've been able to think about ever since you moved in with me. Night after night, you've been lying there across the corridor and I thought about doing this,' he said, kissing the wildly beating pulse below her ear, 'and this…and this,' he murmured as his lips traced a delicious path down her throat while Miranda shuddered with pleasure.

His fingers found the zip at the side of dress. 'This is a dream come true.'

'What else happens in your dream?' she asked with a low, shaky laugh, and Rafe eased the straps from her shoulders until the dress slithered over her skin and fell in a puddle at her feet.

'I'll show you,' he said.

'Remind me why it took us so long to do this,' said Rafe lazily.

Miranda lay within the curve of his arm. Her head was on his shoulder and she was playing idly with the hairs on his chest. Making love to her was supposed to have been a way to get her out of his system, but that didn't seem to have worked at all. Rafe remembered that breathtaking, heart-swelling, bone-melting mixture of passion and tenderness and excitement and a wild, unexpected sweetness, and his arm tightened around her.

'Because it was a very bad idea,' said Miranda, rather muffled against his chest. 'And you don't need to remind me it was mine.'

'It didn't feel bad to me,' said Rafe, stroking the hair back from her face and craning his head to try and see her expression. 'Wasn't it good for you?'

'You know it was. Too good,' she said honestly. 'How am I going to pretend what we just shared never happened?'

'Do you have to? Why can't it happen again?'

She shook her head slowly. 'There's no future for us, Rafe. We both understand that. We want completely different things.'

'We wanted the same thing a few minutes ago,' he reminded her, a smile in his voice. 'We don't have to think about the future. Can't we just enjoy the present?'

Miranda was very still, and he began to hope that she was changing her mind, until she said in a small voice, 'I'm scared. Tonight was wonderful, but it doesn't change what I really want. I'm going to Whitestones and you'll stay in London, and if I get used to nights like this one I'm afraid it'll hurt too much when I go. It'll be too hard to say goodbye, and we're going to have to say that some time soon.'

Rafe was silent. How could he argue with her? The last thing he wanted was to hurt her, and, besides, she was right. They didn't have anything in common. They wanted different lives. Miranda wanted the fairy tale, and he couldn't give her that. The sensible thing would be to admit that this had been a mistake and agree not to repeat it.

But it didn't feel like a mistake when her skin was silky and her hair smelt of flowers and when losing himself in her had left him with an extraordinary sense of peace and a rightness he had never felt before.

CHAPTER TEN

As the days passed, though, it began to seem more and more like the mistake Miranda had called it.

Rafe tried to carry on as before, but it was impossible. He couldn't get the feel of her, the taste of her, out of his mind. Her scent and her softness and her sweetness seemed to be imprinted on every fibre of his being. Now he avoided touching her at all, afraid that if he did he wouldn't be able to stop at taking her hand or resting his hand on her back to guide her through a crowd, but would end up yanking her into his arms and doing something stupid like begging her not to go.

Because she would go. Miranda was stubborn. Whitestones had been her goal all along, and now that it was in her sights she wouldn't change her mind.

Rafe told himself that he didn't want her to. He wanted a clever, sophisticated wife who would be a companion and a partner, who would run his houses for him and entertain and support him as he transformed Knighton's and proved that he was worthy of the legacy his father had left him, however unwillingly. Miranda had no interest in doing any of that. She wasn't what he needed.

No, he had to stay focused. He would find someone else, someone perfect, and forget Miranda and the soaring sweetness they had found together.

'What did you think of Caroline?' Rafe leant aside to let the waiter deposit a plate in front of him.

It was an evening towards the end of that long week, and they were in an Italian restaurant. Rafe suspected Miranda was no hungrier than he was, but they had both ordered a bowl of pasta. The reception they'd attended had finished by eight o'clock, and neither wanted to go home and endure terrible tension there, where nothing stood between them and the memories of the night they had shared. At least when they were out and surrounded by other people they could preserve the illusion that things were normal. Whatever normal was nowadays. Rafe wasn't sure he could remember.

Miranda picked up her fork. 'Caroline? Which one was she?'

'She's a solicitor. Blonde, attractive.'

'Oh, yes.' Miranda shrugged and took a mouthful of spaghetti. 'A bit bland.'

'What about Helen, then?'

'She'd be very high maintenance.'

'How on earth did you work *that* out?'

'You can tell. You don't get to be that driven without becoming completely neurotic on the way.'

Rafe blew out an irritated breath. 'You don't like any of the women I think might be suitable!'

What did he expect? Miranda wondered crossly. He was always doing this, speculating about the women he might ask out the moment she was gone, wondering which of them would make him the best wife, as if she was supposed to *care*. He seemed determined to rub her nose in the fact that there would be another woman sleeping with him, loving him, waking up to the warmth and security of his body and to the smile in his eyes.

She should never have asked him to make love to her. What a stupid, stupid thing to do! If she'd thought about it, she could have guessed what a wonderful lover Rafe would be. It wasn't as if she hadn't known that he had a lot of experience. She understood now why all the beautiful women he had dated and had been photographed with had worn such wide smiles. She must have seemed woefully inexperienced in comparison, she thought miserably. No wonder he was so keen to find someone else now! He clearly couldn't wait for her to leave.

Still, there was no need for him to go on and on and *on* about it. Rafe had been like this all week, she thought, exasperated. Everywhere they went, he wanted to know what she thought about the women they had met. He probably thought she had fallen in love with him since they had slept together and was terrified now in case she forgot the terms of their agreement.

He ought to know her better than that. Miranda's lips thinned. The constant reminder that he was looking forward to a future without her was grating on her nerves, and she was brittle with the effort of not seeming jealous.

'I don't have to like any of them,' she said, unable to keep the tightness from her voice. '*I'm* not proposing to marry any of them.'

'You could be a bit more supportive, though,' said Rafe grouchily.

'Supportive?' Miranda's voice rose as temper frayed the edges of her control and she dropped her fork onto her plate with a clatter. 'I've *been* supportive! I've dressed up like a doll every night. I've turned up at endless stupid parties and let you paw me in public. How much more supportive do you want?'

'That's what I'm paying you for,' said Rafe, nettled. 'Quite a considerable sum, in case you've forgotten.'

'Believe me, I'll have earned every penny!'

'I'm surprised you didn't ask for more if it's been that awful,' he snapped, still smarting from that pawing comment.

'If I'd known what it was going to be like, I would have done!' Miranda glared at him, her eyes a glacial green. 'What do you think it's been like, Rafe, having you parade women in front of me all week while you look them over like horses? I'm surprised you didn't ask them to open their mouths so you could inspect their teeth! Did it ever occur to you to think that I might find that all a bit *humiliating*?'

Rafe's expression hardened. 'That was the deal.'

'The *deal* was that you pretend to be in love with me, not that you ignore me completely. You've been in a foul mood all week. You haven't laid a finger on me, barely addressed a word to me and made sure everyone knew you were bored stiff by me. You did everything but dump me publicly! And you dare accuse *me* of not being supportive!'

A muscle was jumping in Rafe's jaw, and his eyes were colder than Miranda had ever seen them. 'You're never happy, are you, Miranda? You don't want to sleep with me again, but you complain when I don't touch you. You want to run away to Whitestones, but you don't want me to meet anyone I can be happy with.

'Or maybe that's the problem?' he went on savagely as she sat there, cold with shock and fury. 'You don't want anyone to be happy because you don't know *how* to be happy. You're too repressed to let yourself go and have a good time, or, if you do, you immediately run away the moment happiness rears its ugly head.'

'That's not true!'

'Isn't it? Why are you so desperate to go to Whitestones? OK, it's somewhere you were happy in the past, but I'm betting its real appeal is the fact that there's no one there who might ask you to be happy now.' Rafe looked at her contemptuously. 'You haven't got the guts to go for what you really want, Miranda.'

'Oh, I don't know about that,' said Miranda, pushing back her chair, picking up her plate, and tipping spaghetti right over his head. 'That was *exactly* what I wanted to do,' she told him.

Rafe leapt to his feet, swearing, and the low hum of conversation in the restaurant stopped abruptly as every head swivelled to stare at him as he stood there, spaghetti dripping from his hair and off his shoulders.

'What the—? What are you *doing*?' he snarled, his face white with fury.

'Just taking your advice,' Miranda said. 'And you know what? You were right. Now I've stopped being repressed and started doing what I want, I feel really happy! Thanks so much for the tip!'

Tugging the exquisite diamond ring from her finger, she dropped it deliberately into his fettuccine. 'While I'm doing what I want, I'll give you that back, too. You can send a cheque to me at Rosie's.'

'The hell I will!'

Belatedly becoming aware of the fascinated stares, Rafe grabbed Miranda's arm and jerked her towards him so that no one else could hear. 'We had an agreement,' he reminded her in a savage voice.

'And I'm keeping it,' she said, so angry she could barely bite out the words. 'You wanted me to be the one to end our engagement, and I'm ending it.'

'Not like this! You've made me look a fool!'

'I have, haven't I? Oops,' said Miranda coldly. 'Never mind, they'll all feel sorry for you now. That's what you wanted, isn't it? They'll be queuing up to console you for losing your boring, miserable, *repressed* fiancée!'

Wrenching her arm free, she snatched her bag off the back of her chair. There was a deathly hush at the surrounding tables, and she put up her chin and looked around at the faces, agog at the excitement of the scene.

'I never liked that suit,' she said, and walked out, leaving Rafe ridiculously and furiously alone in the middle of the restaurant, his hair clogged with sauce and spaghetti straggling from his shoulders.

* * *

Miranda set the ladder against the wall and tested it gingerly. It was very wobbly, and she bit her lip. She hated heights at the best of times, and climbing a rickety ladder set on uneven ground hardly counted as one of those. But she would have to get up there somehow. The gutter was blocked, and would have to be cleared, or the problem would just get worse. And there was no one else to do it.

There was no one else to do anything. She had been at Whitestones nearly a month. She had unpacked the hire car alone and carried everything across the field alone. She had made the house habitable alone. She had cleaned and cooked and tidied alone. She had pulled water and started the generator alone.

She walked on the beach alone.

She went to bed alone.

Still, it was beautiful, every bit as beautiful as she had dreamed all those years in London. Miranda woke up to the sound of the sea every morning. She walked along the cliff and breathed the clean air, and told herself that she was happy.

But she wasn't. She was lonely.

There was silence and space and light, but there was no one to talk to, no one to laugh with, no one to exasperate her.

No one to make her heart jump just by walking into the room. No Rafe.

You don't know how to be happy. His words echoed endlessly in Miranda's head, and her heart twisted with pain. She had been happy when she was with him, but it was too late to realise that now. Even if he hadn't wanted such a different life from hers, there was no way Rafe would ever forgive her for that plate of spaghetti.

She shouldn't have done it, Miranda knew, but she had been so angry and so hurt. And so bitter with herself for wilfully ignoring all those sensible warnings in her head that had kept telling her it could never have worked. Why hadn't she listened to them? Rafe was too handsome, too charming, too desirable for a girl like her. She had *known* that he could never love her.

She had thought he liked her, though. Miranda couldn't bear to remember the contempt in his voice that night. The truth had come out then. He thought she was boring, repressed, cowardly… Oh, God, here came the memories again, like a cruel fist grasping and tearing at her entrails.

Miranda took her hands from the ladder and covered her face with them instead. She tried to breathe through the pain, but still the hot tears came, squeezing out from beneath her lashes, no matter how desperately she willed herself to hold them in. She mustn't cry. She *mustn't*.

If she started, she would never stop.

Drawing a shuddering breath, she brushed the treacherous tears from her cheeks furiously. In the end, Rafe had sent her a cheque by express courier the very next day, and she had gone straight out to hire a car, ignoring Rosie's pleas to wait and talk to Rafe when they had both calmed down. She had never been back to his house to collect her clothes. None of them really belonged to her, and she wouldn't wear any of them again anyway. Instead, she packed up her few possessions and drove down to Whitestones, and she had been here ever since.

And now she was here, she would make the best of it. She *would* be happy.

Determinedly, Miranda grasped the ladder, and set her foot on the first rung. She would survive. She would be happy. She would unblock that gutter. She could do this.

She got as far as the sixth rung before the ladder lurched to one side and she froze with a whimper of fear. Her heart was hammering in her throat, and all she could do was grip the ladder and stare fixedly at the brickwork, too terrified to move in case she dislodged the ladder further.

Now what? She was either going to have to stay up this

wretched ladder for ever, or fall off, in which case there would be no one to find her. It had been stupid to try and do this alone.

'Are you on your way up, or your way down?'

The achingly familiar voice made Miranda start so violently that the ladder jerked away from the wall momentarily and she gasped with fear even as her heart leapt with incredulous joy.

Rafe. *Rafe.* He was here and suddenly the world was glorious again—or it would be if she dared look down to see him.

'I'm stuck,' she said.

'No, you're not,' said Rafe. She felt him take hold of the ladder and steady it. 'I've got you,' he said. 'Come on down.'

Biting her lip, Miranda inched her hands lower and forced her right foot to reach down for the rung below. Very gradually, she made it down to the next rung and then the next, and the next, and the last two were easy, although her knees were shaking when she finally had both feet back on the ground and she could turn and look at Rafe.

It might have been him that was making her knees weak. He was dressed like a million other guys in jeans, with a jacket over his shoulder and a long-sleeved cotton shirt pushed casually above his wrists, but he looked so gorgeous and vital and *immediate* that it was all she could do not to throw herself at him and shower him with kisses while she patted him all over to make sure that he was real.

He *was* real. 'What on earth were you doing?' asked Rafe conversationally, as if the last time they had spoken they hadn't flayed each other with bitter, angry words.

'Trying to unblock a gutter,' said Miranda, trying desperately to steady her reeling senses. She was so happy to see him that she couldn't think straight. 'What are *you* doing?'

'Trying to unblock my life,' said Rafe. 'And bringing you a present.'

'A present?' she echoed blankly. Perhaps this *wasn't* real?

Why, when she had dumped a plate of spaghetti on him, would he bring her a *present*? Why would he come at all? Her heart was hammering again, but this time with frantic hope. 'What sort of present?'

'Wait here and close your eyes.'

It felt so surreal that Miranda simply did as he ordered. She sat down on the verandah steps and closed her eyes, tipping her face back to the sun and enjoying its dazzle behind her eyelids.

Please don't let this be a dream. Please don't let him be gone.

But, no, there were footsteps on the wooden verandah behind her. She felt him crouching down beside her, and the next moment a soft, squirming body was placed gently in her lap.

Miranda's eyes flew open to see a puppy sprawled across her knees. It had huge paws, floppy ears and a velvet soft coat, and it was licking her hands and wriggling with pleasure.

All the breath leaked out of her. 'Oh…' Her throat was so tight, it was all she could say for a while. She looked up at Rafe. 'He looks just like Rafferty,' she managed, but her voice was cracked and constricted and she was very close to tears. All of her childhood, she had dreamed of a puppy just like this one.

'He's an Irish Setter,' said Rafe, obviously pleased at her reaction. He sat down beside her on the step and reached over to scratch the puppy's head. 'I couldn't get a mutt in case it didn't look right.'

'Is he really for me?'

'He is, but you might not want him when you see what he eats! I warn you, he chews everything. I only had him in the house for about an hour this morning, and he's already ruined two pairs of shoes, my best tie and the remote control for the television!'

Miranda laughed shakily and lifted the puppy so that they were nose to nose. 'Are you very naughty, darling?' she asked him, and the puppy's long pink tongue lapped eagerly, trying to reach her face.

'I thought he'd be company for you,' said Rafe, watching her face alight with laughter. 'It must be lonely down here on your own.'

Her smile didn't fade, but some of the light seemed to go out of her. She glanced at him, confused by his thoughtful gesture, even more confused by her own reaction. He had given her a beautiful puppy, and gone to all the trouble of finding one that would look like her beloved Rafferty. How could she not be grateful to him? She ought to be ecstatic. But if he thought she needed company, that meant he wasn't planning on staying.

Well, what had she expected?

'It's really kind of you, Rafe,' she said. '*Thank* you. I love him.' She fondled the puppy's ears. 'I don't deserve him after I threw spaghetti all over you.' She glanced at him. 'Is it too late to say that I'm sorry?'

'Not if I can say sorry too,' said Rafe. 'I think we both said and did things we regret that night, but in one way it couldn't have worked better. After that spectacular end to our engagement, I got plenty of sympathy!'

Miranda made herself smile. 'So our plan worked?'

'You could say that.'

'Well…good.' She kept her smile in place. It was enough that he was here, she told herself. He had brought her a gorgeous puppy, and was prepared to be friends again, even after she had behaved so appallingly. What more did she want? 'So, have you found a fiancée yet?'

'I have,' said Rafe, and her heart sank lower than she would have believed possible when she was holding a wriggling puppy. 'At least,' he qualified, 'I've decided who I want to marry, and now I've just got to persuade her to agree. That's why I'm here, in fact. I need your advice.'

'You want *my* advice?' Miranda gaped at him. Didn't he *remember* that terrible row?

He nodded. 'I thought you'd be the best person.'

'I'm surprised you'd want advice from someone boring and repressed!' she couldn't help saying, unable to keep the hurt from her voice.

'You were never boring, Miranda,' said Rafe gently. 'I never called you that.'

'You implied it. You said I didn't know how to be happy.'

'*Are* you happy?'

Instantly her chin came up. 'Of course I am. I've never been happier. I've got everything I've always wanted, especially now I've got *you*,' she added to the puppy, who was struggling to get off her lap. Carefully, she lifted him up and set him down at her feet, where he gambolled a little way before tripping over his paws and flopping down onto the grass.

She smiled brilliantly at Rafe and gestured out at the sea, which was glittering silver in the afternoon sun. 'How could I not be happy here?'

'Ah,' he said, and looked away. 'I'm glad.'

Miranda glared at his profile. Honestly, how obtuse could he be?

'Of *course* I'm not happy,' she said crossly. 'I'm *miserable*. Is that what you wanted to hear?'

He turned at that. 'It is, actually.'

His eyes held a smile, but Miranda couldn't look at him. Biting her lip, she jerked her gaze away. 'Probably serves me right for dumping spaghetti on you,' she said.

To her horror, tears clogged her throat without warning, and she had to swallow painfully before she could produce a bright, bright smile. 'Anyway, I'm glad you've met the right woman for you,' she managed after a moment. 'What's she like? Is she nice?'

'Well, *I* like her,' said Rafe. 'She's different. She prefers dogs to people, can you imagine that? She doesn't like being in the city and she hates dressing up and going to parties.'

As his words sank in Miranda's heart began to thud. It was slamming steadily, painfully against her ribs, and, hardly daring to believe that it wasn't a cruel joke, she turned her head very, very slowly to meet his eyes once more.

They were dark and blue and very warm. 'She wears dull little suits and ties her hair up,' he went on, 'and if you watched her dealing with a photocopier, say, you would think she was really repressed.'

Miranda moistened her lips. 'I can't think why you would want to marry someone like that,' she said unsteadily.

'The thing is,' Rafe confided, 'only I know that when she lets down her hair and takes off that suit, she's the wildest, most exciting, most beautiful woman I could ever hope to meet. Making love to her was a big mistake, in fact, because once I'd done that, I knew that only she would do.

'The thing is,' he said again, his voice very deep and low, 'nothing is quite right without her. *I'm* not right without her. I tried to be. I tried as hard as I could. I told myself that I could easily love someone else, that marriage was better approached practically rather than emotionally. That's what I wanted to feel. It's what I felt I *should* feel. The trouble was that once she'd gone, I realised that it wasn't what I *did* feel.'

Hope was gripping Miranda's heart so tightly it was almost painful, and it was all she could do to breathe past the constriction in her chest. 'What did you feel?' she asked huskily.

'I felt that I had found the one person I didn't know that I had been looking for all these years,' said Rafe quietly. 'The one person who could make me feel complete.'

Reaching out, he took Miranda's hand at last. 'I didn't think it could be you, Miranda. There seemed to be too many reasons why it shouldn't be you, but it *is* you,' he said.

His fingers curled around hers, his clasp warm and strong and infinitely reassuring. 'Dad always complained that I never stuck at anything. I thought I had to stick at Knighton's to prove him wrong, but I don't. All I need is to prove to you that I love you.'

Rafe lifted their clasped hands to his lips and kissed her knuckles. 'I'm asking you for the chance to prove that I can stick with you for ever.'

'Rafe...' Miranda's heart was so full she couldn't speak. She could just stare at him, her eyes shimmering with unshed tears as happiness seeped like sunshine along her veins.

'I'm not asking you to leave Whitestones, Miranda. I know what it means to you. If you—and the dog—' he added, nodding at the puppy which was snuffling inquisitively through the long grass, 'will have me, I'll move down here too. It's not as if I'm short of a bob or two. I don't need to work. I could unblock those gutters for you.'

He was babbling, Rafe realised, and he made himself stop. His fingers tightened around hers. 'What do you think?'

'I think,' she said slowly, 'that you need Knighton's more than you think you do, Rafe. Your father entrusted the company to you, and you need to fulfil that trust.'

'But then I'd have to be in London, and you would hate that. You need to be here, at Whitestones.'

'I need you more,' said Miranda, and reached for him as the tears spilled over at last. 'If London is where you are, that's where I need to be too.'

'Miranda...' Rafe held her away from him just long enough to look down into her face and see the love in her eyes before he pulled her into his arms for a long, sweet, almost desperate kiss.

'Are you sure?' he asked raggedly when they broke for breath. He rested his cheek against her shining hair and held her tightly. 'It's not just about you. You've got the dog to think of now, remember.'

Miranda laughed shakily. 'There are parks in London,' she reminded him, 'and we can come down here at weekends, can't we?'

'We can.' Rafe pulled back to take her face between his hands and fix her with serious eyes. 'But maybe we need to think about this. I can't ask you to come back when you hate it so much.'

'Well, maybe I don't hate London *quite* as much as I thought I did,' Miranda confessed. 'I've been down here for nearly a month, and, to be honest, I'm dying for a cappuccino!'

Rafe laughed and wrapped his arms around her once more. 'I've missed you so much, Miranda,' he told her with a sigh.

'I've missed you too,' she said, nestling closer, still hardly able to believe that he was there. 'I've been so lonely without you.'

'I'm so sorry for all those terrible things I said to you,' said Rafe. 'I didn't mean any of them. I was just feeling desperate. I wanted you so much, but I knew I couldn't give you the fairy tale *you* wanted. I still can't,' he said seriously, tipping back her head to look down into her face. 'It won't be perfect all the time, but I love you and I need you and I think that as long as we're together, we can get through anything.'

Miranda smiled through her tears. 'That *is* the fairy tale, Rafe,' she said, and she kissed him again.

Much later, they lay on the rough grass together as the puppy clambered over them, licking their chins and chewing their fingers with sharp little teeth.

'Ouch,' said Miranda, laughing, and tugged gently at his ears. 'I had thought I might go back to work, but I can see you might turn into a full-time occupation!' she told the dog.

Rafe lay with his hands behind his head, watching the clouds drifting across the sky. He had discarded his jacket and his shirt was unbuttoned at the neck. 'It's hard to think about work when you're down here,' he said. 'Have you missed it?'

'Sometimes,' she admitted. 'I quite like being in an office with lots going on. And, of course, you never know who you're going to meet when you're at the photocopier!'

He laughed and pulled her down beside him. 'I'm very glad that agency sent you to Knighton's. I might never have met you otherwise.'

'I suppose it wasn't too bad as assignments go.'

'Do you fancy another one?'

Miranda tucked herself into his side and rested her cheek on his chest with a contented sigh. 'That depends what kind of assignment you're talking about.'

'I'm in need of a wife,' said Rafe in a mock businesslike tone. 'It's a permanent position, and you'd have to be prepared to be adored for ever. There are one or two conditions attached, of course.'

'What sort of conditions?'

'You'd have to adore me back,' he told her. 'Oh, and you'd need to wear this every day.' Digging into his shirt pocket, he produced the diamond ring that Miranda had last seen as it plopped into his pasta.

Taking it from him, Miranda turned the ring between her fingers so the diamonds flashed in the sunlight. 'Hmm... sounds quite an interesting job,' she pretended to muse. 'What's the deal?'

'Well, there would be a few details to sort out, but before we go into that I'd need to know if you were available and willing in principle to take the position.'

Miranda smiled as she remembered the last time Rafe had used those words. Then he had been asking her to pretend to love him. Now it was wonderfully, gloriously for real.

'I'm available,' she assured him, slipping the ring back on her finger where it belonged and raising herself on one arm so that she could bend to kiss him softly. 'And very, very willing!'

* * *

It was a perfect day for a wedding. The bride looked like a fairy-tale princess, in a stunning ivory silk creation, swathed in antique lace. A gossamer-fine veil streamed from the tiara she wore in her beautiful hair, and she carried a bouquet of exquisite, creamy yellow roses. Glowing with happiness, she laughed up at her groom, who wore a faintly stunned look, as he if couldn't quite believe she was really his, and his expression when she kissed him made more than one of the guests wipe a surreptitious tear away.

'You look beautiful,' Rafe told Miranda.

'It must be because I'm so happy.' She leant against him with a smile. 'I feel as if my heart is going to burst with it. It was a beautiful wedding, wasn't it?'

'Perfect,' said Rafe, 'for Octavia and Simon. Not for us.'

'No,' she agreed, her smile widening. 'Not for us. Today is everything Octavia has ever dreamed of, and I'm so happy for her, but our wedding isn't going to be like this, is it?'

'Ours will be perfect for us,' Rafe promised. 'It'll be everything *you* dreamed about that day at Whitestones when we walked on the beach together for the first time.'

'Miranda!'

Octavia's voice interrupted them and Miranda turned to see Octavia on the steps, the voluminous skirt of her dress caught up in one hand. Smiling at her sister, she tossed the bouquet straight towards her.

The roses came sailing through the air straight towards her, but Miranda wasn't ready. Caught unawares, she dithered and stretched out her hands too late. 'Oh, no!' she cried, hating the thought of the beautiful roses crashing to the floor.

'Oh, for heaven's sake!' Grinning with affectionate exasperation, Rafe shot out an arm and caught the bouquet just in time. Bowing in acknowledgement of the rousing cheers, he presented them to Miranda with a flourish. 'I believe these were meant for you,' he said. 'You must be getting married next!'

A-brim with happiness, Miranda laughed and took the roses with a kiss.

The dress, an exquisite confection of silk and chiffon, was hanging behind a door, floating ethereally whenever the air so much as stirred. A bouquet of meadow flowers would be delivered in the morning. The champagne was already on ice. That was the extent of the preparations for *their* perfect wedding. Elvira was determined to throw a spectacular party at Knighton Park to celebrate afterwards, but for Miranda and Rafe their wedding day was for them alone.

'Only two weeks,' Rafe murmured in her ear. 'Then it'll be just you and me—and the dog, I suppose. We'll be sitting on the beach with that champagne, just like you dreamed, and we'll be married at last. We'll listen to the sea and, when the champagne is finished, we'll go back to Whitestones to make love all night—and then we'll wake up in the morning, knowing that we've got the rest of our lives to spend together.'

Miranda sighed happily and kissed him again. 'I can't wait,' she said.

JANUARY 2009 HARDBACK TITLES

ROMANCE

Captive At The Sicilian Billionaire's Command	978 0 263 20695 1
Penny Jordan	
The Greek's Million-Dollar Baby Bargain	978 0 263 20696 8
Julia James	
Bedded for the Spaniard's Pleasure	978 0 263 20697 5
Carole Mortimer	
At the Argentinean Billionaire's Bidding *India Grey*	978 0 263 20698 2
Virgin Mistress, Scandalous Love-Child	978 0 263 20699 9
Jennie Lucas	
Ruthless Tycoon, Inexperienced Mistress	978 0 263 20700 2
Cathy Williams	
Cordero's Forced Bride *Kate Walker*	978 0 263 20701 9
The Boss's Forbidden Secretary *Lee Wilkinson*	978 0 263 20702 6
Italian Groom, Princess Bride *Rebecca Winters*	978 0 263 20703 3
Falling for her Convenient Husband *Jessica Steele*	978 0 263 20704 0
Cinderella's Wedding Wish *Jessica Hart*	978 0 263 20705 7
The Rebel Heir's Bride *Patricia Thayer*	978 0 263 20706 4
Her Cattleman Boss *Barbara Hannay*	978 0 263 20707 1
The Aristocrat and the Single Mum *Michelle Douglas*	978 0 263 20708 8
The Children's Doctor's Special Proposal *Kate Hardy*	978 0 263 20709 5
The Doctor's Baby Bombshell *Jennifer Taylor*	978 0 263 20710 1

HISTORICAL

The Rake's Defiant Mistress *Mary Brendan*	978 0 263 20957 0
The Viscount Claims His Bride *Bronwyn Scott*	978 0 263 20958 7
The Major and the Country Miss *Dorothy Elbury*	978 0 263 20959 4

MEDICAL™

English Doctor, Italian Bride *Carol Marinelli*	978 0 263 20909 9
Emergency: Single Dad, Mother Needed	978 0 263 20910 5
Laura Iding	
The Doctor Claims His Bride *Fiona Lowe*	978 0 263 20911 2
Assignment: Baby *Lynne Marshall*	978 0 263 20912 9

MILLS & BOON®
Pure reading pleasure™

JANUARY 2009 LARGE PRINT TITLES

ROMANCE

The De Santis Marriage *Michelle Reid*	978 0 263 20473 5
Greek Tycoon, Waitress Wife *Julia James*	978 0 263 20555 8
The Italian Boss's Mistress of Revenge *Trish Morey*	978 0 263 20556 5
One Night with His Virgin Mistress *Sara Craven*	978 0 263 20557 2
Wedding at Wangaree Valley *Margaret Way*	978 0 263 20558 9
Crazy about her Spanish Boss *Rebecca Winters*	978 0 263 20559 6
The Millionaire's Proposal *Trish Wylie*	978 0 263 20560 2
Abby and the Playboy Prince *Raye Morgan*	978 0 263 20561 9

HISTORICAL

The Shocking Lord Standon *Louise Allen*	978 0 263 20650 0
His Cavalry Lady *Joanna Maitland*	978 0 263 20651 7
An Honourable Rogue *Carol Townend*	978 0 263 20652 4

MEDICAL™

Virgin Midwife, Playboy Doctor *Margaret McDonagh*	978 0 263 20483 4
The Rebel Doctor's Bride *Sarah Morgan*	978 0 263 20484 1
The Surgeon's Secret Baby Wish *Laura Iding*	978 0 263 20485 8
Proposing to the Children's Doctor *Joanna Neil*	978 0 263 20486 5
Emergency: Wife Needed *Emily Forbes*	978 0 263 20487 2
Italian Doctor, Full-time Father *Dianne Drake*	978 0 263 20488 9

MILLS & BOON®

Pure reading pleasure™

FEBRUARY 2009 HARDBACK TITLES

ROMANCE

The Spanish Billionaire's Pregnant Wife	Lynne Graham
The Italian's Ruthless Marriage Command	Helen Bianchin
The Brunelli Baby Bargain	Kim Lawrence
The French Tycoon's Pregnant Mistress	Abby Green
Forced Wife, Royal Love-Child	Trish Morey
The Rich Man's Blackmailed Mistress	Robyn Donald
Pregnant with the De Rossi Heir	Maggie Cox
The British Billionaire's Innocent Bride	Susanne James
The Timber Baron's Virgin Bride	Daphne Clair
The Magnate's Marriage Demand	Robyn Grady
Diamond in the Rough	Diana Palmer
Secret Baby, Surprise Parents	Liz Fielding
The Rebel King	Melissa James
Nine-to-Five Bride	Jennie Adams
Marrying the Manhattan Millionaire	Jackie Braun
The Cowboy and the Princess	Myrna Mackenzie
The Midwife and the Single Dad	Gill Sanderson
The Playboy Firefighter's Proposal	Emily Forbes

HISTORICAL

The Disgraceful Mr Ravenhurst	Louise Allen
The Duke's Cinderella Bride	Carole Mortimer
Impoverished Miss, Convenient Wife	Michelle Styles

MEDICAL™

A Family For His Tiny Twins	Josie Metcalfe
One Night with Her Boss	Alison Roberts
Top-Notch Doc, Outback Bride	Melanie Milburne
A Baby for the Village Doctor	Abigail Gordon

MILLS & BOON®
Pure reading pleasure

FEBRUARY 2009 LARGE PRINT TITLES

ROMANCE

Virgin for the Billionaire's Taking	Penny Jordan
Purchased: His Perfect Wife	Helen Bianchin
The Vásquez Mistress	Sarah Morgan
At the Sheikh's Bidding	Chantelle Shaw
Bride at Briar's Ridge	Margaret Way
Last-Minute Proposal	Jessica Hart
The Single Mum and the Tycoon	Caroline Anderson
Found: His Royal Baby	Raye Morgan

HISTORICAL

Scandalising the Ton	Diane Gaston
Her Cinderella Season	Deb Marlowe
The Warrior's Princess Bride	Meriel Fuller

MEDICAL™

Their Miracle Baby	Caroline Anderson
The Children's Doctor and the Single Mum	Lilian Darcy
The Spanish Doctor's Love-Child	Kate Hardy
Pregnant Nurse, New-Found Family	Lynne Marshall
Her Very Special Boss	Anne Fraser
The GP's Marriage Wish	Judy Campbell